A
Harlequin
Romance

OTHER
Harlequin Romances
by JOYCE DINGWELL

Many of these titles are available at your local bookseller,
or through the Harlequin Reader Service.

For a free catalogue listing all available Harlequin Romances,
send your name and address to:

HARLEQUIN READER SERVICE,
M.P.O. Box 707, Niagara Falls, N.Y. 14302
Canadian address: Stratford, Ontario, Canada.

or use order coupon at back of book.

SISTER PUSSYCAT

by

JOYCE DINGWELL

HARLEQUIN BOOKS   TORONTO
WINNIPEG

Original hard cover edition published in 1971
by Mills & Boon Limited.

© Joyce Dingwell 1971

SBN 373-01772-3

Harlequin edition published April 1974

1772   Printed in Canada

CHAPTER ONE

'SISTER PUSSYCAT,' called Ann Mary, 'why is the sky up?'

She was the youngest one, and Catty had allotted her Ann Mary because already there was an Ann. Two more, in a way. An Ann and an Anne with an E.

'But our Anns without the E comprise the bottom and the top,' had pointed out Mrs. Chester, the Manager's wife, when she had presented the children to Catty, 'Ann Mary, five, and Ann, rising fifteen.' She had not dwelt on in-between Anne with an E because there were twelve other in-betweens as well. There were fifteen girl wards.

But it was Ann Mary of the fifteen who had started 'Sister Pussycat'. Previously the housemothers had gone under Aunty, the Manager, Mr. Chester, had explained, adding to Aunty the Christian name. It gave, so the Board considered, a family touch.

'No,' Catty had said, 'no.' Then emphatically, '*Not* Aunty, please.'

Mr. Chester, delighted to have snared a housemother when the Positions Vacant columns of the Sydney dailies fairly wept for applicants, particularly certificated nurses, when, in despair, he ultimately had had to advertise abroad, had suggested, 'Matron, then? Sister?'

'Sister will do, Mr. Chester.'

'And why not, my dear, when you've reached that praiseworthy state, yet not, by your obvious youth, ever practised the stage, or very little of it?'

'Thank you,' Catty had said, letting him think that that was the reason because the truth was too painful to tell, that truth that having been an aunt and being that aunt no more she never wanted to be an aunt again. Not after Gaby and Georgie.

They had been her adoped brother's two small daughters, Gabrielle and Georgina, and she had loved them as she had loved Roger, their father. She would have loved Lilla, too, Roger's beautiful wife, had Lilla allowed. Love spilling over, Roger had frequently teased.

But it had dried up now ... at least she hoped it had. Fondness, yes, perhaps even affection, but love only tore at the heart.

When Roger had died so young, too young, his widow Lilla had put it concisely and coolly.

'This is the end of your affair, Catriona, with my children.'

'Roger's children as well,' Catty had reminded her dully, not believing what she had heard.

'Roger is dead. Then even had you been *really* related ...' Lilla's voice had trailed off significantly.

'There never was any secret that I was adopted,' Catty had cried hotly.

'Nor any secret how delighted you were about that. I can tell you now that Roger is gone how nauseating I always found it.'

'My delight,' had flashed Catty, 'or Mother remembering me when she died?' There had been a small bequest.

'*Mother?*' Lilla had sneered.

But Catty had known it was really that money, the money that Roger had been pleased over, but his wife ...

She had said sensitively that Lilla could have the money ... it was still intact, Roger had invested it for her ... after all, Lilla would need it now that she had Gaby and Georgie to support.

'Not I,' Lilla had smiled.

'What do you mean?'

'I mean I'm marrying again, Catriona, and this time there'll be no need to worry when an upstart takes what she should never have been given.'

'Lilla!'

'It's true.'

'Lilla, I just offered you my money.'

'And I just told you I won't need it. Carl' ... a little smile ... 'is rich.'

'Carl? Not that man who was here that day I called?'

'Yes.'

'You're marrying him?'

'I just said so.'

'After Roger?'

'Listen, Catriona, Roger and I were washed up ages ago.'

'But what about Gaby and Georgie—?'

'What about them?'

'Does – does Carl love them?'

'Not love again.' A sneering laugh.

'*Does* he?'

'Well enough.'

'How much is that?'

'Sufficient to put them in a good boarding school, which Roger never would do.'

'He didn't want them away.'

'Well, they're going now, and where *you* won't be able to visit them. We all leave for America at the end of the month. The end' ... Lilla had said again ... 'of the affair.'

'Can I see them?'

'No.'

'Before they go, Lilla?'

'No.'

'Just to say goodbye?'

'I'll say it for you.'

'Lilla—'

'No.' Lilla had waited a vicious moment, then, in her final deprivation, she had stacked all the stored-up jealousy and resentment of years. 'No, *Aunty* Catty!'

Catriona had walked out of the house and back to her flat.

'No,' she had said to Mr. Chester a month later, 'not Aunty. Sister.' It was thousands of miles away, it was Australia, not England, but there must be no more spilling of love.

That it was Australia was only incidental. Anywhere would have done. But the advertisement had preferred a graduate from a children's hospital, which she was, it had needed her at once, which she needed. She had applied, been accepted and had gone, then later she had come. Come to Camp Universe, Emu Heights, New South Wales – to be even more explicit, to the recently opened young female section of Camp Universe: Sky House.

'Sister Pussycat,' called Ann Mary again, 'why is the sky up?'

It was the youngest who had suggested Pussycat. Catriona was beyond her and Catty wasn't so nice as Pussycat, she said.

'But I mightn't be nice,' Catty had warned the fifteen of them.

'You're nicer than Aunty Beryl, she huffed and puffed up the stairs; and she got scotty.'

'Aunty Enid always said "My daughter Phyllis never did that," ' rankled Dorothea. 'I hated that Phyllis.'

'Aunty Mavis,' said Anne with an E, 'was yuk.'

'Yuk,' the rest of them agreed.

'Girls!' Catty had been very reproachful, and at once they had apologized, for, as far as they were concerned, it had been love at first sight. Not that with Catty, though, she would not permit love even at second sight, but she did permit Pussycat instead of Catty or Catriona, but no . . . *not*, do you hear me, girls? . . . Aunt.

'It was Aunt-ee,' Ann Mary said.

'Just as we call him Uncle,' explained one of the inbetweens. 'He's a nice uncle, though he's really a doctor.'

'Who is, Janet? Who are you talking about?'

'Doctor Jasper. He's outside looking in. Looking at you.' Janet nodded to the common-room window of the villa-type building, one of several such erections.

There *was* someone there. Uncomfortably, Catty got up. She had only been here a few days and she was still feeling her way around.

'Is he really a doctor?' she asked.

'He's Doctor Jasper.'

'Did someone send for him? Is anyone sick?'

'He would come, anyhow,' advised senior Ann. 'He's on the Board.'

'You mean – he just visits here, with no—' She had been going to say 'No warning.'

'Yep.'

'Yes, Anne.'

'Yes, Sister Pussycat,' Anne said ... and said it just as the man who had been outside now came in.

'Pussycat?' That was his first word.

'I can explain that.' Catty stepped forward.

'Good. The Sister, of course, explains itself.' There was a tightness to the rather long sensuous mouth of the distinctly long man confronting Catty. 'Right, girls, give me ten minutes with—' A pause. 'Ten minutes with *Sister*, then back to where we stopped last time.'

Someone called eagerly, 'Chapter Three.'

'The spaceship with Bettina in it,' someone else called, 'has just taken off.'

'That's it,' he nodded. 'Ten minutes.' He nodded again. 'Watch the clock in the hall.'

But Catty herself watched the retreating heels of the fifteenth child, watched those heels rather nervously. Then she turned to the man watching her.

'Please sit down, Mr. – that is Doctor—' Well, she could scarcely call him Uncle, could she?

'Either will do,' he said coolly. 'The name is Jasper.'

'So the girls said.'

'Oh, yes, females, even the young ones, would know that; they're born busybodies, and their insatiable personal curiousity is aided and abetted by their cool, controlled, calculating little minds.'

9

She was completely taken aback by his plain dislike of her sex, but Catty still found words.

'I should think coolness and control would be desirable traits,' she said, 'and surely calculation is wiser than recklessness.' Already she knew she disliked this long doctor.

'Perhaps ... but the humbug they delve in, the spite and mischief. The noisiness. No doubt they know already I'm David Jasper, aged—'

'Please let me find that out from them,' Catty cut in thinly. When he did not answer, she said, 'You seem popular with them for a man who dislikes the female of the species.'

'Yes, I dislike it,' he said quite frankly, 'but not them *as children*. As potential women, perhaps, but not at this green stage.'

'Feeling like that it's a wonder you accepted them.' The Chesters had told Catty that these fifteen were the first females ever to be embraced into Camp Universe.

'*I* didn't,' he replied, 'but nine others did.' He paused 'There are ten on the Board.'

'And you were outvoted?'

'Yes.'

'A disappointment for you.'

'A catastrophe for Universe,' he emended.

A silence grew between them. He looked at his watch, then said, 'Five minutes gone already. I'd better not waste any more time.'

'It hasn't been wasted, Doctor Jasper, you've let me know where you stand.'

'And you ... *Sister*, not Aunty, I believe ... where do you stand?'

'How do you mean? You know I've been appointed here as house-mother—'

'Mother?' He gave a short laugh. 'Not even Aunt. What is this all about Sister Something-or-Other?'

'Sister Pussycat.' She was red with embarrassment and hated him for it. 'The children have nicknamed me Sister

Pussycat. I know it's absurd, but—'

'Absolutely absurd.'

'My name is Catriona. I said it could be Catty, but the youngest one preferred Pussycat.'

'Yet prefaced with Sister?' he inserted.

'Yes.'

'Why?' he asked.

'I prefer to give no reason.' Her chin was up.

'That's all right, Sister, the reason is obvious. I shouldn't have asked. You are proud of your nursing status. Well, fair enough.' Another pause. *'But you also wish to stand aloof, out of any family circle, hence you are not Aunt.'*

She did not answer.

'Well,' he demanded, 'don't you?'

'If you mean by that that I wish *not* to be involved—'

'I mean it.'

'Then yes.'

'Good. We know where we stand. *Both* of us serving this place, *both* uninvolved.'

'In your case female section, of course,' Catty came in.

'Agreed. I have no objection to the male division. I should think' . . . he had narrowed keen grey eyes on her . . . *'you* would have no objection, either.'

'Why should you think that?'

'Young and pretty and very conscious of that fact.'

'You're impertinent, Doctor!'

'And you are indiscreet, Sister, to say that to a Board member. However' . . . a yawn . . . 'don't let it fret you, you won't get dismissed.'

'Those nine votes to one, Doctor Jasper?'

'Plus a disastrous labour shortage in Sydney. From your accent, I gather Chester had to try distant fields.'

'I'm English,' she said stiffly.

Another silence grew. Once more he broke it. He said, 'You won't see much of me. I'm responsible for the health of the Camp, but they're mainly bouncing little

11

beggars.'

'Is today's visit to check to see if they still bounce?'

'No. A serial I'm reading whenever I get an opportunity.'

'*You* are reading?'

'I could add that I'm interested as well.'

'With Bettina in this spaceship?'

'I will admit I would sooner it were Bob.' Actually he smiled, and it took some of that long look away from him. 'I will admit, too,' he went on, 'that I can overlook what my audience will be one day, that is while they are children. So' . . . He spread his hands.

'Ann is rising fifteen, almost out of childhood,' dared Catty, 'Dorothea is close behind her. Do you wish me to remind you to start disliking them soon?'

He was getting up from the chair, moving to the door to let in the fifteen. 'Another female trait,' he mused hatefully, 'acidity.'

She disliked him so much any disliking he had of her and her sex couldn't have matched it. Her hands were closed tightly as the girls came running in.

'Uncle David!' – So, as he had said, they knew his name.

'Uncle David, when you were six instead of thirty-six, did you—' For a moment, across the room, his eyes taunted hers.

She turned and went outside the villa. She stood in the garden, waiting for the visit to end. While she waited she tried to shut her ears.

But still it reached her, the saga of Bettina, the daring space-woman, Bettina who should have been Bob, the story told to girls who should have been boys. And who would be passed over presently to Sister, who he unmistakably wished was not here at all. One vote to nine, he had said, and he had lost.

He came out at the end of the chapter, surrounded by the fifteen. He got into a small car Catty had noticed drawn up on the drive and was shrilly and fondly fare-welled. The Camp Universe was large, but surely not large enough to require a car to cross from the boys to the girls, or even from the hospital, Catty remarked to her bunch.

'But he just doesn't look after us, Sister Pussycat, he's the doctor of Emu Heights as well, and Emu Heights goes right from the river up to the mountains,' senior Ann said.

Since her arrival Catty had studied her location and wondered at the expanse of it ... and the sheer love-liness.

Forty miles from Sydney, along the Kurrajong Road, suddenly the Camp Universe sign indicated a winding track, and after some miles the Camp opened up. It was nothing like a camp, that was just its name, it was some-thing much more imposing. Its sprawl of buildings rested on a smallish mountain with four surrounding saucers of valleys, but it was on the top that Catty first had stood ... and caught her breath. In the dim distance Parramatta discarded its dusty suburbanism to become an enchanted purple city, then the little hamlets with their chequered sections of brightly-hued market vegetables took over right to the sandy rim of the twisting green ribbon that was the Hawkesbury River. After that, the hills of Kurrajong climbed up, all patterned in citrus groves dripping yellow and golden loot. Looking next from the east to the west, the Great Dividing Range, of which this lesser height was a contributing foothill, flaunted its Blue Mountains, the nearer greys and greens changing, as the heights and miles accumu-lated, to a shouting, almost impertinent postcard blue.

Catty had turned quite beauty-dazed, to Camp Uni-verse itself. She had learned its history.

A philanthropist with unusual ideas had bought the mountain and erected the master building. A man of vast dreams, he had wasted no time on local standards.

Already the camp was Camp Universe, so the master building was called Horizon Hall.

He had lived to add River Lodge, Earth Court, Valley Hostel, Grass Gully, other vital living names. Sky House he had not been able to wait for, but he had desired to have females, too, since the universe included them, and he had left a request that if this happened, it should be called Sky House. 'For,' Mr. Chester had related respectfully, standing beside Catty, 'who is higher, Our Founder said, than womanhood?'

Catty had been impressed then. Now . . . after a certain visit . . . she compressed her lips at the thought instead.

The money that the benefactor had left had not been sufficient by latter-day standards to permit females – that was, until this year. Then more wherewithal had been raised, the deciding question put to the Board and eventually approved . . . by nine to one, Catty knew now . . . and the first intake accepted.

'Not entirely successfully,' Mr. Chester had grieved.

'There are always teething troubles.'

'Perhaps, but our house-mothers were not the right type. Camp Universe is not the place you can pop out of to do some fancy shopping, and being a restricted location we seemed to get a restricted applicant. Now you, Miss Quentin—'

'Am a migrant who wouldn't know where to go if she got out,' suggested Catty smilingly.

'Well, I suppose being a newchum would persuade you to settle for a while before you tried your wings, but apart from that you're young, you're not dried up. They' . . . in apology . . . 'were my good wife's words. She said, "She may not have had house-mother experience but she's not dried up. Children must have love."'

'I'm sure I'll do my best.' Catty had pretended to be looking at the scene again. She needed this job, in fact she had to have it, her money was exhausted, otherwise she would have told Mr. Chester how wrong Mrs. Chester was. Where love spilled over, eventually it must come to an end. Hers had.

Mr. Chester had told her about the boys. Not so many of them, but more than the girls – some twenty odd. They occupied Earth Court and Grass Gully.

'Then the other accommodation, River Lodge, Valley Hostel, is vacant,' Catty assumed.

'Never at week-ends,' and a smile now. 'You see, when the money petered out, the Government stepped in, and in return for their financial aid we take in many sectors of the young public they send up to us for school vacations or for Saturdays and Sundays.'

'What kind of young public?'

'Orphanage inmates in need of a change... police boys' club members ... selected school kids in need of the break as recommended by headmasters ... aboriginal welfare nippers. Sometimes doctors ring us up with an SOS. We take them all in and receive Government remuneration for their week-end or week stop. It all helps.'

'The place appears self-supporting,' Catty commented.

Mr. Chester had glowed. 'Indeed it is. This is a great growing area. We supply our own eggs, milk, fruit, vegetables, bacon, sometimes even sell some. We have a dairy man, a pig man, a vegetable man. An outside orchardist gives free advice and supervision. The permanent boys work under the men in their spare time for a small but welcome wage, each to his own choice.'

'The boys have to leave at a certain age?'

'Only because the local school cuts its grades at sixteen, and it's too inconvenient to travel daily to a higher education.'

'So then the children, the permanent ones I mean, have to return to their first orphanage?'

'Mainly they're not orphans. Sometimes I wish ...' Mr. Chester had sighed. 'An orphan is easier,' he had explained. 'Those with one parent, or worse still with two conflicting parents, are harder to handle, poor little mutts.'

'I think,' Catty had commended, 'that you handle them wonderfully, you and Mrs. Chester.'

The manager had looked pleased at her praise. 'You can place them as soon as they arrive,' he had related. 'The eyes that follow Mrs. Chester belong to those missing a mother ... either dead or cleared out ... and the eyes that follow me need a dad.

'Here' ... he had been leading Catty into Horizon Hall, large, rather official-looking, the place of honour on the wall allotted to a portrait of Our Founder ... 'is where each new influx begins its Universe experience. The permo kids, of course ... the permanents, I should say ... know the ropes already. But the week-enders or vacationers arrive in the Universe bus and are instructed to take from that large bench always laid in readiness two sheets, a pillowslip and two towels each. The rest after that is up to them.'

'Cleaning, you mean?'

'No, only each cot, its bedmaking. We have a char. But tidiness is sought after. We have a tidiness dormitory award for each batch.'

'What about meals?' Catty asked next.

'We have a cook and an offsider, and the kids collect their meals at the hatch and take their dishes back. That's the boys, of course. For the girls I'll pass you over to Mrs. Chester.' He had taken Catty over to the Chester bungalow. Here, over tea, Mrs. Chester had added her notes.

'Your job will be to supervise Sky House, dear. Add the woman's touch.'

'I think the girls would have had that already with you.' Mrs. Chester was undoubtedly a warm person.

'When I have time,' the manager's wife admitted, 'which is far too seldom. When you go into Sky House you'll see you have an adjoining bedroom with a window that looks out on the dormitory.

'We don't ring bells for meals here, food is practically always on, so the getting of the children to the diningroom will be your responsibility. Anyway, their stomachs will prompt them to remind you.'

'Have they far to go to school?'

'Only down the valley. They cut their own lunches. Doing it that way you're sure of getting no complaints.'

'The youngest one, too? You told me you had a five-year-old.'

Mrs. Chester said that she expected the smallest one got help. 'But you'd better supervise Ann Mary's own concoctions or she'd take all sugar sandwiches.'

They laughed.

'Am I to watch their general health?' Catty had asked next.

'Yes, dear. I have been doing that, but not being a nurse I fear I've been worrying our Doctor Jasper far too much.'

Catty had accepted that then. Now she would have said that it would be no worry *unless it was a girl.*

She had been taken across to Sky House, and, school being finished and the girls back again, presented to the fifteen, from Ann Mary up to Anne. After an Aunty who was scotty and an Aunty who trotted out her daughter Phyllis and an Aunty who was yuk ... she must stop them saying that ... they had looked at her, small, fair, not so far away from them in years not to understand, and loved her at once.

But not Catty. Never. Never any more.

The girls gathered around her now that Doctor Jasper had gone. They begged for a walk, and when she agreed spread out on each side of her, the two Anns in pride of place on left and right arm. Well, thought Catty, remembering her minister in London, that was right. The Reverend Mr. Flett always had said that he intended serving the young and the old, trusting that the in-betweens would look after themselves. Catty hoped her in-betweens were doing that now.

'I love you,' said Ann Mary blissfully. 'You're the same as my grandmother.'

Not exactly exuberant about that, Catty supposed that at least she should be pleased about Ann Mary's next: 'Except you're not dead.'

A little deflated, Catty asked Ann Mary about her mother, remembering from the histories she had scanned briefly last night that Ann Mary did have a mother. But all Ann Mary would say was: 'She's not dead.'

Anne, rising fifteen, was edged out of her pride of place by Dorothea, next in age, who suggested eagerly that they visit the swimming pool. Catty had not seen it yet, but Mrs. Chester had told her it was a fine pool and built entirely through street stalls. 'Jams and aprons,' she had said rather vaguely, or so Catty thought as she looked at the glittering blue Olympic-sized reservoir of crystal water, with its surrounding changing houses, its springboards and starting blocks. She wondered how many aprons and jams.

Dorothea said, disappointed, 'The boys aren't in.'

It was the first indication that Catty had had as yet that a senior girl was growing up, and she looked sympathetically at Dorothea. She was as tall as Ann, nearly as matured, and certainly never a gentle dreamer like their eldest girl. Her history, she recalled, had mentioned a mother.

'It can't be their swimming period,' she suggested. 'When does Sky House plunge in?'

'We don't.'

'Don't go swimming?'

'Not so far, Sister Pussycat.'

'Then we'll see about that,' Catty resolved.

As it was spring, and the breeze on the mountains quite sharp, there was no marked jubilation, except in Dorothea ... definitely growing up, Catty now decided ... who asked when Sister Pussycat did see about it could she have a bikini.

'We'll see about that, too, dear.'

'If I don't have one, I won't learn,' stated Dorothea.

Catty in her surprise disregarded Dorothea's rebellion.

She said, 'Learn? Surely you already swim?' Dorothea looked sulky. 'Well, don't you?'

'No.'

'Me neither, Sister Pussycat.'

'Nor me.' . . . 'Nor me.'

In the end only two of the fifteen could, and this was Australia, island in the sun!

'We'll see about it,' Catty said again.

'And the bikini?' Dorothea hoped.

As they walked past the manager's bungalow, Mrs. Chester came out, and Catty sent the girls on.

'How is it going, Sister?' the older woman asked.

'Slowly,' Catty admitted. 'Getting to know fifteen children can't be done in a day. But I've learned something just now that has disturbed me. Only two from Sky House could be permitted in the pool.'

'They can't swim, you mean. Yes, that could be true. They were mainly city-dwellers.'

'But there are city pools, and in Sydney there are beaches.'

'A lot of these girls have had the responsibility of younger children, quite often they're the eldest of a string of children, and probably haven't had the time as well as the opportunity to learn.'

'There's time and opportunity here. I must put it to the Board. When do they meet?'

'Only once a month. The last meeting was just before you arrived. However, any problems can be taken to David Jasper.'

'Doctor Jasper?'

'Yes.'

'But why? Is he some special member of the Board?'

'No, not exactly, but he's the only resident member, well, resident, anyway, as near as Emu Heights, the rest are Sydney men, so it was agreed that he settle any immediate questions that arise.'

'Then I would say the girls won't swim,' sighed Catty.

'Oh, come,' smiled Mrs. Chester, 'he's not as bad as that.'

'On the subject of *females*, he is.'

'I've not been involved with him except on the subject of males,' admitted Mrs. Chester with the warm intrigue that arises in small settlements. 'What would have caused it, do you think – a jilt?'

Catty agreed that that could be.

'I'd still try him,' said the manager's wife. 'Swimming is very important. He was up today, so it's unlikely, unless we send for him, that we'll see him for the rest of the week. He has a very big practice. But you could go to the surgery at Emu Heights. Nine to ten.'

'At Emu Heights?'

'Yes. It's quite a pleasant track through the bush.' She glanced sympathetically at Catty. 'I wouldn't let this swimming business dismay you, dear. The girls have been here very little longer than you have, and everything, as regards Sky House, is still at a trial and error stage. The other house-mothers were barely unpacked before they were packing. After they saw our remote situation any small interest they might have had – though frankly I doubt that they ever had any real interest, not those women – fled. So don't be put off by what isn't done, take it as a challenge to be done, Sister.'

'Thank you, I will.'

Catty found more to be done in the meal room later.

Ann had come to her and said, 'Are we eating before or after the boys, Sister Pussycat?'

'Why not together?'

'We never do.'

'But why not?'

'We just haven't.'

Dorothea called, 'Oh, Sister Pussycat, could we?'

Catty privately could not see why they hadn't eaten together right from the beginning. After all, Our Founder could not have meant such a separation of the two young sexes, not in such a lofty dream as a universe.

'We'll see,' she said firmly again.

However, it was too late to try it today, so she super-intended the passing out of the laden plates through the hatch by Cooky's offsider, accepted her own plate and ate quickly, seeing as she did that a lot of table manners were going to need help, then took her plate right into the kitchen.

Cooky was plump and good-tempered. 'You only have to leave it at the hatch, miss, and Don will take and scrape it and put it in the dishwasher.'

'You seem to have all conveniences,' said Catty.

'Yes, we're pretty well done by, both by the Government and donations. I've no complaints, except, perhaps, that it's an all-time job.'

This was the opening Catty needed.

'Then why two meal sittings, Cooky?'

'Boys *and* girls,' Cooky reminded her.

'Well, why not together?'

Cooky stared at her. 'Never thought of it,' he admitted, 'I just naturally made two batches of it. Of course' . . . dubiously . . . 'there could be high jinks.'

'Over steak and kidney and creamed rice? Oh, I'm sorry, it's just that I hardly think—' Catty smiled at the cook; she had a nice smile and it took away any of the sting he could have felt about the stew and pudding.

'You mean it's not exactly wine, women and song,' he grinned. 'I see your point. And I see mine, too, now you come to mention it. Even though I more or less always have an open kitchen it would be nice to get things done for the night in the one fell swoop.'

'Breakfast, too. They're all away for lunch, aren't they?'

'On schooldays, yes.'

'Well, we'll think about it, shall we? Meanwhile, I'll get my girls out and leave you to prepare for the male onslaught.' She collected her fifteen and took them across to Sky House.

It was getting dark, and the lights from the valley were

opening up like blossoms. The homesteads to the farms and orange groves seemed to be laid out in geometrical pattern, they made a glowing mosaic. Far in the distance Parramatta was a blurred band of fire. Only where the river curved was there any pause in the shining lights.

It was too beautiful to go inside, but fifteen wards had to be bedded at hours suitable to their ages.

After half an hour of Ludo and Snakes and Ladders, Ann Mary was tubbed and tucked in. From then on it was a continual programme of small girls being checked that they had dried themselves in the creases, 'gone' before they went to bed, then kissed and God Blessed. Only Anne and Dorothea remained.

Anne, in whom Catty already saw the sure signs of a future nurse, did the final rounds of blanket adjusting and putting out of lights, while Dorothea, second eldest, not so dedicated, or if she was then certainly travelling in another channel to Anne, just stood by the window and stared out. What was she thinking? Catty wondered, trying to remember back to her own fourteen.

'Time, darling,' she said presently.

Dorothea came back from her world of stars. 'You will try about a bikini, Sister Pussycat?'

'It would be better to swim first.'

'But if anyone saw me in an awful one-piecer . . .'

'The champions wear one-piecers.'

'But I'd die, I swear it, I'd die of shame!'

'Look, Dorothea, if you learn to swim I promise you a bikini. Though I suppose if you have one Anne—'

'Anne's different. She wouldn't care. I do care, I care terribly. Please, Sister Pussycat!'

'I've promised,' Catty reminded her. 'If you learn to swim, we'll go ourselves to choose the bikini.' She felt that learning to swim vindicated a bikini.

'Oh, Sister Pussycat!' Dorothea kissed her fervently and went off to the bathroom.

'Dry in the creases,' Catty called out automatically, 'and "go" before you get into bed.'

22

She said the same to Anne, who was last to depart, then she went in, as she had with the others, and kissed and said God Bless. The eldest girl was plainly astonished, she murmured, 'I've never had that said to me.'

'Perhaps your mother thinks you're too old now,' smiled Catty.

'I never had it said to me at all,' Anne said.

'Goodnight, pet.' Catty put out the light and came out again. There was a hardness in her throat, but she swallowed it and put on her desk light. She intended to take out the girls' histories and go through them again.

But before she did so she stood at the door and looked down once more on the shining night valley, beyond the valley to Parramatta; beyond that was Sydney, she thought, the world.

Camp Universe, Our Founder had called it, but just now Catty thought more humbly about the world.

Not Australia, where she was, nor England, where she had come from, but America, America where Gaby and Georgie were, where her heart was. And the ruins of her love.

She turned sadly back to her desk.

CHAPTER TWO

WHY had she loved them as she had? Why, thought Catty, still not starting on the girls' files, does a rose bloom? It was as simple and needless to explain as that.

She had been eight when Mother had taken her, a funny little eight, she recalled wryly, straight tow hair, grave eyes and teeth that stuck out. They still did a little, but Mother had had a dentist see to the worst of that. Roger had stepped in before they were absolutely straight, saying that men quite liked little rabbits, and whatever her 'brother' had said had been right with Catty.

She could remember obeying Matron's summons to her office that morning, thinking drearily: 'Here it goes again.' For the Home had never succeeded in 'placing' her. 'It's not you, dear,' Matron, who had been kind, she remembered, had said, 'It's your age. People like small ones.'

'I was small once.'

'Yes, but you—'

But, Catty knew now, you had things that people, quite nice people, people who were doing a lot more than other people, did not really want to have to bother about. Like teeth that stuck out. Like eyes that needed correction. Like sticks of legs. Like – the people had been kind and had handed over sweets and patted her head ... and taken someone else.

But *that* time it had been different. The tall, sweet-faced woman had said, 'Catriona – how pretty. Will you come and live with us?'

The big boy ... sixteen, she had found out later ... had grinned and said, 'Puss-puss.'

Always that had been a signal for battle, but not now. She had loved her 'mother' and her 'brother' on sight.

24

It had been a sorrow to her that she could not be Catriona Forbes instead of Quentin. But perhaps Roger would wait for her, then ask her to marry him if she hurried and grew up.

Roger had not waited, he had married Lilla, and since everything Roger did was right, Lilla was right. – Only Lilla was wrong.

Mother had known that, too. She had said before she died: 'I'm leaving you something for yourself, Catty. I know Roger would look after you, but—'

Lilla had been terribly angry. She even let Catty know her anger so Catty could guess how Roger was feeling. But he had remained adamant, probably for the first time with Lilla, and had invested Catty's money, but little lines had crept into his smiling boyish face, grey had streaked his brown hair.

He still kept his door well open to his 'sister', though, his children available for 'Aunt' Catty's love. And how she had loved them, small Gabrielle, smaller Georgina. It must have been her 'unbelonging' that had made the love well up in her like it had. She had loved Mother but Mother had had to leave her. She had loved her brother, but Roger had gone with Lilla. So all her love had come to the children.

It never had occurred to her how Lilla had thought of that love until Roger had died far too young and Lilla had said what she had: 'The end of the affair.'

It seemed now to Catty that she was back in the Home once more, being called to Matron's office and thinking drearily: 'Here it goes again.'

Only . . . taking out the files . . . she wasn't back there. *She* was the Matron, at least Sister. If anyone did any placing, or advised it, she did it. A little half-hysterical laugh escaped her. How could the unplaced place? For that's what it finally had come back to, Catriona Quentin, Unplaced.

But so long as the place where Gaby and Georgie were, that 'good school' that Lilla had spoken of, was right, then she was right. Just so long as her girls had what Roger would have wanted his daughters to have, she said to the file that read: Grant, Anne Dinah, fourteen, that's all she cared. For all her love was there.

She studied the page.

Anne had both parents, but the parents had split up. There had been an argument as to who would get Anne, but the way Mr. Chester had written it down unofficially for Catty it seemed patent that the argument had been who was going to have to have her.

Catty sighed, and took up the next file. It was Dorothea and rather the same story.

Deborah next. Thirteen. One of seven. Father had abandoned mother and family. In the end it had got too much and Debby's mother had had to seek help. Four of the seven had been taken, the Government promising to look after them until better times, and Deborah had been one of them and had come here.

Heather, also thirteen, was the aboriginal child, originally brought down to Sydney from the far west to receive medical treatment. The after-treatment entailed a year of check-ups, and as there were other children in the family the parents had returned until such time that they could take Heather home with them. Catty noted where Mr. Chester, the manager, had written in a margin that Heather had come better dressed and better pocket-moneyed than all the rest. She was financed, and financed handsomely, by the Aboriginal Welfare Board.

Adrienne's mother – Adriene was twelve – had left home one day and never come back. Her husband had found he could look after the four boys but not the one girl.

The Child Welfare had removed Margaret from parental 'care' after being called in to investigate by the school doctor. Catty bit her lip here.

Helen, eleven, was an orphan. Catty was pleased that she had received a different surname from Smith or

Jones, she had always been grateful to Matron for naming her Quentin, even though later she had yearned to be called Forbes.

Nora, another split family victim, had been tried by several institutions. Could Camp Universe break through?

On, on Catty went. She would have read into the small hours, she smiled some time later, had Anne not come apprehensively to the door of the office and confessed, 'I forgot to go, so I'm going now. I'm sorry, Sister Pussycat.'

'That's all right, darling, only remember next time.'

'Aren't you going to scold? Aunty Mavis did. She was y—'

'That's not a kind word. If you use it I *will* scold. Hurry up now, then back to bed.'

Putting away Mr. Chester's histories, Catty went to bed as well.

No need for an alarm clock with children. They awoke with the birds, and though Catty could hear senior Anne trying to hush them so as to let Sister Pussycat sleep, Anne, too, must have wanted Catty to get up, for she started a series of noisy yawns and wake-up ho-hums.

Accepting defeat, Catty rose and went into her personal shower. When she had dressed she came out and examined the children's dress. They were in the tunic of their valley school, a simple green cotton with a white collar. They looked fresh and sweet, and she could have kissed every one of them.

'The boys have finished breakfast,' Dorothea told her.

'How do you know, Dorothea? Do they always eat at this time?'

'I watch for them,' Dorothea said . . . then flushed. When Catty appeared not to notice, she reminded her, 'You said we might all eat together, Sister Pussycat.'

'Yes . . . but not breakfast, I think.'

'Why?'

'Because breakfast is a hurry-up, get-going meal. When you're both married one day, Anne and Dorothea . . . and all of you . . you'll see what I mean. Your husband will be hurrying off to the office and your children will be hungry. You'll have everything to do at once.'

'I don't want to be married,' Anne said. 'I want to—' Her eyes dreamed.

'I don't want to be married either,' came in Dorothea. 'It doesn't work.'

'It does, darling. Most often it does.'

'It's yuk.'

'Sister Pussycat doesn't like that unkind word,' advised Ann Mary. 'Can we go over to breakfast now?'

Catty collected them all and they went across. This was actually Catty's first supervising breakfast at Camp Universe. On her previous few days school had been closed, and the children not needing to be strictly on time since there had been no lunches to cut had gone casually in the small friendship groups in which they usually gathered. But today classes waited in the valley, and the bell, Ann Mary informed Catty, would go clang-clang at ninety o'clock.

As Catty entered the big dining hall she saw that as well as the breakfast waiting to be handed through the hatch, one of the large tables had been laid out with platters of sliced buttered bread then a selection of fillings. There was white paper to wrap up the finished sandwiches, slab cake for play-lunch and a bowl of oranges.

Breakfast was oatmeal, boiled eggs and a mug of cocoa. It was eaten briskly, for some of the sandwich fillings were favourites, and the early comers got the lion's share.

But Catty considered this unfair for slow eaters so restricted the favourite filling to two sandwiches only . . . also not spread too thickly.

A few grumbles greeted her decree, but they took it fairly well, and Catty sat back sipping the coffee Cooky had brought her and enjoying the sight of fifteen assorted heads bent busily over fifteen lunch bags.

She remembered . . . too late . . . Mrs. Chester's warning about their youngest member. By the time she got to Ann Mary's side she saw the entire contents of the sugar pot being emptied on to one slice of bread.

'No, Ann Mary,' she said firmly. Ann Mary's lip dropped. 'Well, one sugar sandwich this time, but only one. And half that sugar.' She shook it off. 'Now, what will we put on this other? Tomato? Egg?'

'Sugar.'

'Yes, but only on one, and thinly.'

Ann Mary began to cry. She cried like five-year-olds do, loudly, heartbrokenly.

'Next,' advised Anne knowledgeably, 'she'll sob.'

Catty hoped not, she had had experience in the wards with sobbers. They could go on for hours. It was distressing to the listener and sometimes dangerous to the one who cried.

She tried diversion. She tried bribery. But she could see that Ann Mary's crying rhythm had been put into motion, and the spasm would have to wear itself out. There was no question of the little girl going to school, not in this emotional state, so Catty nodded the others away, then sat with Ann Mary until gradually the sobs lessened, then stopped.

'We'll go for a walk,' she told the youngest. 'Would you like that?'

'Yes, Sister Pussycat.'

'We might even take a sugar sandwich. Just this once.'

Typical of children, Ann Mary said, 'I don't like those things. I'm not eating those things any more. I like bread and termartersauce.' Oh, dear, Catty said to herself, seeing heartbroken sessions to do with tomato sauce, here we go again!

But not now. Now they were going to take that pleasant walk through the bush that Mrs. Chester had

29

spoken of that led to the Emu Heights surgery of Doctor Jasper. Catty consulted her watch and saw that if they left soon they should fit in with the doctor's consulting hour.

Ann Mary was all smiles at the prospect. Without any doubts the girls loved their doctor, rankled Catty, whereas *he* ... She took the youngest's hand and set off.

It proved a delightful walk. It rimmed an orange grove and crossed a little creek over which had been arched a tiny Japanese bridge. They stood on the bridge a while launching bark boats, listening to the tiny plash the water made as it gurgled over lucky stones. Gnats traced flight patterns in the still air and crickets sang. It was all too lovely to leave to visit a doctor.

But the fact of her non-swimmers weighed heavily on Catty. She allowed a final boat to be launched, then they started the small climb to the tiny village where Doctor Jasper had his surgery.

There was one patient waiting, and she said chattily that another patient was now with Doctor. She talked with Catty while Ann Mary inspected the pile of magazines.

When Doctor Jasper brought his patient out and nodded to the next one, Ann Mary greeted him fondly and received a smile and a wave in return. Then David Jasper inclined his head coolly to Catty.

It was not very long before the patient was out again and calling goodbye to Catty as well as the doctor.

'Will you come in, please.' Doctor Jasper was treating them professionally, and too flustered to stammer out that her visit was not a medical one, Catty took Ann Mary's hand and entered the surgery.

Here, Ann Mary must have seen the examination couch, stethoscopes, various necessities, and recalled instances of other such rooms that she had disliked. Ominously the lip drooped.

But before it finally fell, a barley sugar was plopped

into her mouth, and Doctor Jasper began gravely examining one of her fat brown curls and saying, 'I think you'll be all right.'

Instead of sobs, Ann Mary went into peals of laughter.

'Is she the patient?' David Jasper asked Catty quietly.

'No. You see—'

'How would you like to play with my dog Bimbo?' The doctor opened the back door to the surgery and indicated a large, amiable Labrador, who actually smiled, or it seemed like it, at Ann Mary's cry of joy. David Jasper settled the pair with a dog biscuit and another glucose comforter, then shut the door again.

'Yes, Sister Quentin?' he asked.

But all at once to her extreme embarrassment Catty could not find opening words. She sat pink-cheeked and discountenanced.

'Where is the pain?' he inquired formally. There was a silence, but her expression of distaste must have answered him, for he added stiffly, 'Other than the pain of sitting opposite to me.'

'It's not me . . . I mean it's not—'

'It's not I? No need to bother about being correct, Sister, just tell me why you came instead of sending for me. There's no charge involved. I'm the Camp's honorary medical adviser.'

'As well as the Board member to whom one comes in between Board meetings. You make the interim immediate decisions.'

'So we're getting somewhere,' he said drily. 'You haven't come because it's me or it's I who is ill, nor any of your wards, but on a Board matter.'

'Yes,' Catty said.

He got up and brought across a paper cup of coffee; he had one of those instant machines that dispense with a turn of a tap. It surprised her in such a small surgery.

'Ah,' he said, reading her surprise, 'but patients come

rather a longer distance than usual. I find it helps to relax over a cup after travelling citrus miles.'

'Citrus miles?' she queried.

'The miles around the orange groves. Although they appear geometrical, they're often tortuous shapes ... or at least the roads winding between them are.'

She commented curiously, 'It's a very small surgery, and you haven't many patients. I've been told it's a big practice, but it doesn't appear so. Can you really exist in such a humble position?'

'I exist,' he assured her. He drank some of his own coffee, then explained, 'Mostly my practice is attendance out of the surgery. Only locals find their way here, and, as you remarked, there are not many of them.' He looked down on his desk. 'Only three today, as a matter of fact. But I'll be away the rest of the day anywhere from the river to the mountains. Citrus growers, pig raisers, poultrymen, what-have-you. But in case you're worrying as to how I'm doing, I'm doing nicely, thank you.'

'I wasn't worrying,' she said.

'Good. Then shall we get on to what brought you here? You say it was not your wards?'

'No. I wanted to ask something of you.'

'Yes?'

'The swimming pool,' she began.

'Yes?'

'Was it intended for boys only?'

'When it was built I would say it was, we had no girls then.'

'But you had them in mind – I mean' ... in annoyance as he blandly shook his head ... 'I mean Our Founder had them in mind.'

'Ah, yes, Our Founder.' He gave a thin smile.

There was quiet for a while.

'You don't agree with Our Founder?' she asked.

'On the contrary, I'm sobered by his dream. "Those who seek his memorial look around." All that.'

'But don't let your eyes fall on the girls.'

'You're perspicacious, Sister Quentin.'

'I would be a blind fool if I couldn't see that.'

He downed the last of his coffee. 'Why have you come? Oh, I know it's the swimming pool, but what is it exactly you want?'

'Do the girls swim or not?' she asked bluntly.

'I don't know. I've never inquired of them. Do they?'

'No,' she said hotly, 'no, they don't. Only two of the fifteen, and for someone who comes from a cold country where the pursuit of that sport can only be indulged in several months of the year, I'm anything but impressed.'

'Please go on,' he encouraged. 'It's good to hear home truths.'

'The girls can't swim. Even Anne, rising fifteen, can't swim.'

'What is it you want?' he said hatefully. 'Water wings?'

'I want permission to start them on lessons.'

'You have it.'

That instant capitulation took her by surprise and her expression showed it.

'Didn't expect that, did you?' he grinned. 'Go ahead with your lessons. Only' ... pushing aside the coffee cup ... 'who will give them? I know no one up here and I hardly think the Board with their present overheads would employ a teacher, and I haven't time myself'

'I would teach them.' She had the satisfaction of seeing his surprised look.

'You're qualified?' He put it barely.

'Not every race is won by an Australian.'

'I deserve that,' he said. He got up and filled new paper cups at the dispenser. 'Please go on,' he said sincerely.

'I feel it's very important. You' ... appealingly ... 'must feel that, too.'

He did not speak at once, but when he did his voice was serious

'I do feel it, and I thank you for bringing this to my

attention. It's very essential that every one of these girls learns to swim. But before you decry their inability and our failure to right that, I must remind you that they've been here very little longer than you have.'

'I know,' she nodded, 'and there've been teething troubles. Mr. Chester told me.'

'Good, then I needn't elaborate.' He sat back. 'Go ahead with your classes, Sister Quentin, I give you permission on behalf of the Board. See Tony Williams. He looks after the boys. Though, of course' . . . a dry laugh . . . 'you two have discussed this already.'

'I haven't met Mr. Williams.'

'You surprise me.' His eyes taunted hers.

'Then you must be surprised. I've been far too busy.'

'But you will remedy that.'

'If you say so. Why is it so essential I discuss the swimming matter with him?'

The doctor gave a shrug of impatience 'Times, of course. You can't have the two batches in together.'

'Why not?' Catty's cheeks flamed. After all, this was Camp Universe, and in a universe there were men and women. She felt impatient with the segregation that seemed to enclose the place.

'Because,' he said clearly, 'the boys can all swim, and like all boys they indulge in rough-house, and until the girls can look after themselves it would be much safer.' He paused. 'Sufficiently answered, Sister Quentin?'

'Yes,' she said, humbled.

'Well, that's all.' He half-rose to go to the door to bring in Ann Mary.

'There is a little matter,' she stammered. He did not speak, but he raised thick curved brows and she told him: 'Bathing suits.'

'Bathing suits?'

'Yes. It doesn't appear they have any. Perhaps their parents—'

He brushed that aside. 'One parent perhaps . . . two . . . with luck three. The rest.' He shrugged. She was silent,

34

and he went on, 'I gather you want me to O.K. the purchasing of bathing suits?'

'Yes.'

'I think that can be managed.' He actually smiled at her, and, after a nervous pause to make sure he wasn't preparing another barrage, she smiled back.

'Why,' he asked presently, 'is the little one not at school?'

She related the sugar episode, and he broke in, 'So you rewarded her tantrums with a day off?'

'It wasn't exactly like that.' Again they were going to do battle, she thought wretchedly. 'The child was over-wrought. Anyway' ... defensively ... 'it did good. She's turned her back on sugar sandwiches.'

'Interesting,' he remarked. 'What is the chosen filling now?'

Abysmally Catty said, 'Tomato sauce.'

Her head was down, and the first she knew of his reaction was his hearty guffaw. It bellowed around the room, and she looked up, saw his face, heard the laughter – and laughed, too.

'Tomato sauce,' he said, and laughed again.

Ann Mary opened the door and peeped in. She could see nothing to laugh at, not the sort of things children laugh at. Sorry for grown-ups, she shut the door and returned to Bimbo.

Encouraged by his mood, Catty told him she had been reading up the girls' histories, as supplied by Mr. Chester. 'But what about their medical histories?' she inquired.

'I can't give them to you.'

'I don't know why,' she said indignantly, their moments of shared laughter forgotten. 'After all, as their nurse I should know.'

'I can't give them to you,' he said again with heavy patience, 'because I don't know the histories myself. They've only been here several weeks, and, because of a mishap, they came without any medical charts. I don't know whether they've had mumps, measles, what-have-

35

you. I don't even know if they've been diphtheria-immunized.'

At her look of shock he said, 'Records are being compiled now. The influx was put on us in a hurry. All these girls are girls who couldn't be absorbed elsewhere. The Department did a remarkable job gathering them up and delivering them here, and they're having the records done as fast as they can. But they're an extremely busy section, as you can appreciate, and lately suffered a fire that put them back no end. Everything has to start from taws. It's unfortunate, and it could be disastrous, but that's the position.' He spread his hands.

Catty understood the problem, but she also knew how sometimes a child can miss out on what should be availed to it, either through unusual circumstances in the home, or even parental neglect. She looked up to say how gravely she considered it, then saw his face and knew he considered it gravely too. She did not say it.

'Well' . . . he did get up this time . . . 'I must be on my rounds. Can I take you home?'

'No, thank you, the walk is charming.'

But Ann Mary, called in from the garden, did not want to go home. She had decided she would like to go to school after all. She had remembered that it was Sand Pit Day. She liked that.

'You have no lunch, darling.'

'There is,' said Ann Mary craftily, 'a tuck shop.'

'I brought no money.'

Ann Mary looked steadily at David Jasper.

'Well,' he said, reaching in his pocket, 'this is a fine reward, I must say, for emptying the sugar pot.'

'I won't ever any more,' promised Ann Mary.

'The tomato sauce bottle?'

'I don't like that stuff,' said Ann Mary. She looked blissfully at the twenty-cent piece she had won herself and planned, 'Dog biscuits.' Evidently she had sampled Bimbo's.

'Oh, darling, no!' called Catty.

'Better that,' advised David Jasper drily, 'than twenty cents of sticky toffee. Come on, moppet.'

'Is Sister Pussycat coming, too?'

'Not to school, goose.'

'Where is school?' asked Catty.

'Only along the road. I'll take her. Take you, too, if you've changed your mind.'

'Not changed,' refused Catty. She bent down and kissed Ann Mary. 'Be a good girl, pet.'

'As a matter of interest,' he asked, 'do you do that to the entire fifteen? Or' . . . as she turned to the door, evidently intending not to answer . . . 'is it for the youngest and the eldest only?'

'I haven't worked it out yet. Have you any reason for inquiring?'

'Only the reason that I'm older even than Anne rising fifteen,' he grinned.

'But then,' she pointed out, 'you're a male. Segregation of the sexes, Doctor Jasper. A very important rule.'

Before she could hear his answer, she hurried down the small street and swung back into the bush track.

How beautiful were these citrus foothills; the darkness of the orange leaves was like deep velvet, the scent was heady. Between the symmetrical avenues past which the track twisted before it dipped to the gully with the little runnel and the Japanese bridge again, Catty could see the Great Divide, its Blue Mountains navy blue in front, wispier and merging into a mauve enchantment into the west.

She stood at the wire fence of one of the groves looking with delight at the golden orange treasure massed like a pirate's chest with shining doubloons and gleaming pieces-of-eight. Unable to resist plucking one of the leaves to crush it in her palm and sniff its breath of heaven, she put her hand over the wire.

Instantly there was a low growl, and she withdrew the hand, at the same time apologizing to a black retriever, who had every right to object ... and to someone who stood behind the retriever.

'I'm sorry, I shouldn't have done that. I only wanted a leaf.'

'Kip should have realized that. I apologize on his behalf.' The voice of the man, medium height, young, smiling, held none of Kip's reproach.

'It was still wrong,' she insisted, and went to move on.

'Without your leaf?' he asked, and handed her several attached to the largest orange she had ever seen.

'Only it's not,' he laughed as she said so. 'It's a shaddock. It's for marmalade. When you go home you could make half a dozen pots from a fellow this size.'

'Except that I can't,' she regretted.

'Oh, come, anyone can make marmalade. We ... the citrus fraternity ... put out a leaflet.' He searched his pockets, but in vain, then hunched his shoulders. 'If you'd like to wait ... or even come with me to the house.'

'No, thank you.'

'It would be all right,' he assured her boyishly, 'correct, I mean, I have a housekeeper.'

So he was not married. She said, 'I wasn't meaning that, I was meaning that I couldn't make marmalade, anyhow, because I'd have nowhere to cook it.'

'You board?'

'No, I'm a house-mother up at Camp Universe.'

'Well, now.' The smile that never seemed to be far away flashed on again. 'We're neighbours. Even workmates in a sense.'

'How do you mean?'

'The Camp has its own grove. I superintend it from time to time, tell the boys what they should do, or where they've gone wrong.'

'Oh, yes,' she recalled, 'Mr. Chester told me that there were pig, vegetable and dairy men but that the orchardist gave his advice.' Her voice was warm.

'I like doing it,' he assured her, 'they're fine lads.'

'I don't know them yet. I've been called in for the girls.'

She looked at him closely, waiting for the disapproval she had seen on David Jasper's face.

The smile if possible widened. 'The Camp is a great idea, but it always lacked something. Now it won't lack it.' He gave a little bow.

How pleasant he was. How much easier for her if Doctor Jasper had been smiling and welcoming like this man.

'If you won't come up for a marmalade recipe,' he appealed, 'at least come up for a glass of juice. There's always juice in the fridge. We use our windfalls for that.'

The sun was beating down quite warmly and the idea of a cold orange drink appealed. She said that that would be nice, and slipped under the wire that he held up.

He led her through the groves, so many that she understood why she had not seen his house from the track. As they passed down each symmetrical avenue, he told her what it was, and she was surprised that a citrus grove grew so many varieties. Lemons and oranges mainly, but mandarins, grapefruits, cumquats, limes and the big shaddocks.

There was an experimental avenue, and he showed her how he was trying out a new idea with grafting and 'feathering', which was pollination applied by a feather held in a very steady hand.

'Do the boys learn this?'

'Oh, no, not yet. It needs deep concentration. But they've caught on not to plant nearer than sixteen feet and how to prune an over-exuberant branch. Here we are now.'

It was a pleasant house, pleasant like its owner. It was white and green and wide-verandahed.

'I'm afraid,' the man smiled, 'it won't be juice after all.' He nodded to a tray set out on one of the verandahs, and a woman looked up and called, 'I heard the two voices. It's just drawn. Come and sit down.'

'Mrs. Mallard,' he announced. He looked inquiringly

at Catty.

'Quentin,' she said.

'Miss?' he asked with unabashed eagerness.

'Yes.' A pause. 'Catriona.'

'That's nice.'

'I don't know. The children call me Sister Pussycat.'

They all laughed.

'I'm Bevan Bruce.' He took up the tea that Mrs. Mallard had poured for Catty and asked, 'Milk or lemon?'

'In a citrus grove surely lemon.'

There were cases of oranges at the foot of the verandah steps waiting to be loaded, and Catty noticed how they bore the same stamp on their golden skins as the oranges in the bowls this morning. She said so.

'Of course. I would be very jealous if the Camp ate anything but my own Sunny Wonder.'

'But you must run out of oranges sometimes,' she said, puzzled. 'I mean, here you are with oranges, yet the groves we passed through were only up to hard green balls. Some of the trees were only in blossom.'

'There's always fruit,' he said. 'There's no Cinderella season.'

'But how?'

'Different strains. For instance, the Washingtons crop at another time of the year from the Valencias. Then the Lisbon limes, Marsh grapefruit and Emperor mandarins ... or tangerines if you prefer that name ... each have a favoured month.'

She could have listened all the morning to his citrus talk, but she felt she should get back to the Camp. Although the girls would not return till four, there were many things she wanted to do. She had noticed a hole in Anne's stockings, so feasibly there might be a family of holes to be attended, and though mending was not down on the list of duties she had been allotted, and though Mrs. Chester had mentioned that Universe employed a village seamstress to keep things in order, mending ... strangely, Catty supposed ... was one of the chores as an orphan she had quite liked. It had been the opportunity for retrospection, she supposed, something rather precious in an institution where time to think was rare. She remembered 'Mother's' delight when she had begged to help with the darning after she had joined the Forbes.

'I really must go,' she said, and got up.

'Let me drive you. I intended going to the Camp, anyway. I want to see how the cumquat stood up to the boys' pruning.'

Catty smiled and agreed. She thanked Mrs. Mallard, then followed Bevan out to a utility parked on the drive. Before he put her in, he put a case of oranges at the back. 'Only drop-downs,' he smiled as she murmured an appreciation on behalf of the Camp.

The engine turned over and Bevan steered the ute round a score of curves to the road. Down the hill, nestling in the valley, Catty could see the village where she had visited David Jasper in his surgery. Only he was on his rounds now, rounds that in this big practice would take him all day.

She was disconcerted a moment later to find that one of the calls was the next orchard. Bevan stopped the ute abruptly and called, 'One of the Prentices must be off colour, there's the doc's car. Do you mind waiting, Catriona?'

She supposed life up here was more or less a community life, so how could she mind, especially when she was asked by Bevan, whom already she could call by his name as though she had known him for years, just as he had called her easily and happily 'Catriona'.

'Of course I don't mind, Bevan,' she assured him.

But she did soon afterwards. As Bevan disappeared round one side of the house . . . the Prentice villa was built nearer to the road . . . the doctor appeared round the other side. He came across.

'Enjoying your *walk*?'

'I — I happened to admire Bevan's grove' . . . she

41

noticed how his brows raised briefly at her 'Bevan' . . .
'and after we had tea—'

Oh, why did she feel impelled to explain like this? Her
voice trailed off.

She was relieved that Bevan emerged soon afterwards.

'There must be something sweet about you, like your
oranges,' David Jasper smiled to the young orchardist. 'I
asked if I could give Sister a lift and she said no.'

'As it happens I haven't a sweet tooth,' inserted Catty
stiffly.

'But oranges are acid as well,' he said mildly . . . but
the mildness was only in his voice, and for Bevan, she
knew. Not for her. The eyes turned on her were cold.

'Well, on to tonsils and sinuses,' he said hatefully,
'while you two enjoy yourselves.'

'Mr. Bruce' . . . she was careful to say that this time . . .
'has a supervising job in the Camp grove. I intend to do
some mending.'

'But not on the drive up,' he suggested paternally,
giving her a maddening smile.

Catty bristled, but Bevan Bruce did not seem to
notice.

'He's a fine guy,' he appreciated as they moved off and
up. 'I don't know what Emu Heights will do when he's
gone.'

'Is he going?'

'This is strictly a rural practice, and you can't keep men
like David Jasper in a background like this.' He acceler-
ated to conquer the last steep climb of the Camp.

Before she crossed to Sky House, Catty accompanied
Bevan to the small Camp grove. There were selections of
every type of citrus and the trees looked glossy and
healthy, the soil around them 'kept open' but not deeply
cultivated, for, Bevan said, citrus disliked that.

While they were there they were joined by Tony Williams, the boys' supervisor. It was the first time Catty had
met him, which was not surprising in such a large area,

though, she thought with annoyance, David Jasper had been surprised. Or had it offered one more reason for him to raise his brows at her.

Tony was friendly and seemed co-operative. After Bevan left, he stopped talking with Catty. He was pleased over the girls' inclusion, sorry that it had had a bad beginning. However, that was all over. Teething troubles were always to be expected.

She told him about her non-swimmers, and he took as grave a view of it as she did, but he felt, with Doctor Jasper, that it would be better to have different pool hours until the girls learned to look after themselves.

'For I can assure you,' he grinned, 'I have a pack of young horrors. Nice horrors mostly, but still horrors, especially when they horseplay in the pool. Your dainty Dresdens would be drowned in two minutes.'

'They're not,' Catty smiled, 'which speaks well for the Camp diet. But I see your point ... it's the same as Doctor Jasper's, incidentally.'

'Oh, yes, David would think of that.'

David would think of everything, Catty thought privately and resentfully, but aloud she said, 'I was wondering, too, about meals.'

'Is it that you'd like the kids to eat together?' said Tony perceptively. 'I'd like that too. Some of my fellows badly need a good example.'

'Some of my fellows, too,' admitted Catty with a laugh.

'However,' went on Tony, 'not for breakfast.'

'I agree with you there.'

'It's never a social meal for me,' explained Tony, 'so how could I expect it to be one for them?'

'No, it's a get-up-and-go time, as I told the girls this morning. Do your boys also attend to their own cut lunches?'

'Yes. No grouches then. How did you fare at your first cut-in?'

'Pretty well, except that the youngest emptied the

43

entire sugar pot on to one sandwich.'

'Fair enough,' he laughed. 'I have a terror, Timmy Foster, who puts everything on the one slice.'

'I don't suppose it would harm him,' she said judiciously.

'He doesn't suppose, either, he reckons it would be that way, anyway, once it was inside. But it's not a good example; if everyone decided on it the food bill would soar.' They had emerged from the grove now. 'It's been good meeting you at last, Sister Pussycat.'

'Oh, no!' Catty felt she must protest.

'I'm sorry, but it's public knowledge, you know. The boys' quarters might be on this side of the hill and the girls on the other and never the twain meet, but I've seen quite a few of the horrors looking across at Sky House and giving a miaow.'

'Then they are horrors.'

'Of course,' he agreed wholeheartedly.

'And the week-enders and vacationers?'

'Worse horrors still. But' . . . a grin . . . 'I like 'em.' They had reached Horizon House. 'Coming in for lunch?' he asked.

There was a stocked refrigerator in her own quarters, and Catty decided to eat there, then spend the afternoon sorting out the girls' clothes. She said so, adding that she was glad to have met him, to which he responded warmly that he was glad in return.

As he turned into the hall he called laughingly, 'Appreciate your sugar sandwiches, Sister, if that's the worst you get you'll be doing fine.'

Catty thought so, too. She had a quick light lunch, then got on to the drawers. She liked the work, and the time fairly flew. She was surprised when she heard the return of her girls. Tony was right, sugar sandwiches comprised a very good 'worst'.

But it wasn't just sugar sandwiches. It was worms.

'Worms, Sister Pussycat,' reported Susan furiously, and going to Belinda's cupboard she grabbed everything of

Belinda's she could take up, whirled out of Sky House before she could be intercepted, then down the valley to one of the little runnels that threaded it.

By the time Catty caught her up, three books, a hair ribbon, a pair of slippers, an autograph book and a jigsaw puzzle were swimming in the creek.

CHAPTER THREE

'SUSAN, how could you be so naughty!' Catty only found time for that before she pulled off her shoes and stockings and stepped into the creek. She was vaguely aware as she trod down of a sharp sensation to the ball of her left foot, but in the anxiety of reaching Belinda's treasures before they were born down the valley she barely noticed. Fortunately the stream moved slowly, there had been no rain for several weeks, so she managed to retrieve them all, passing each item back to the watching girls on the bank.

The books had been caught up before much damage was done, but Catty saw, and bit her lip, that they belonged to the school library. The hair-ribbon could be ironed out, the slippers packed with paper and dried, but the album, so dear to a girl's heart, was a sodden mess.

'It had the Beatles' own signatures!' Belinda cried in agony.

'Cut out of a magazine,' sneered Susan, 'and pasted in.' But she sounded a little sobered. And so she must be, Catty knew.

But how to handle the child? Catty was not a teacher, she knew nothing of child pyschology, only what she had learned for herself in the children's wards and that was poor preparation, for a sick child was invariably a placid child, it had no energy to be anything but amenable, poor sweet. Once the demon of health possessed it again, and Catty thought 'demon' deliberately, looking at naughty Susan, the hospital children had been passed on to Convalescent and someone else's care, someone presumably knowledgeable in such matters. Frankly Catty did not know how to handle this.

'Everything can be fixed, Belinda,' she assured the child.

'Fix *her*,' Belinda glowered back.

Anne with an E said unhelpfully, 'The books have marks on them, and you'll have to pay Miss Shipp a fine.'

'Susan will pay that,' said Catty promptly.

'I will not so,' said Susan, 'after those worms.' She turned indignantly to Catty. 'They were on my sandwiches, the worms were!'

'Dead?' asked Ann Mary with interest, 'or squirming around?' She did the actions.

'Ann Mary, be quiet. Girls, gather up all the things. We'll finish this in Sky House.' Catty stepped out and felt a pain in her foot.

'Sister Pussycat, you're all bloody!' Ann Mary cried.

'That's swearing,' called Janet.

'It's not when it's really-truly,' defended Marion.

How had she thought only an hour ago that this was a good post? Catty saw that her foot indeed was bleeding, said that it was nothing, just a scratch, that she would attend to it back at the dormitory, and told the children to move on.

But far less agilely than she had run down to the creek, she came back.

She ordered the girls to remain in the common-room until she bathed the cut, then went to the bathroom and held the wound under the hot water. It stung considerably, but as it still bled she could not judge how deep it was. However, bandaged it felt easier, and she came back to her wards, putting on a severe face that would have sobered them had they not been sobered already.

'Sit down, all of you.'

They sat.

'Although this is only to do with Susan and Belinda ... *I hope* ...' She paused inquiringly, and they all, including the miscreants, nodded. 'Well, although it's their affair I still feel you should be present to realize what a wicked thing wilful destruction is. Destruction like throwing things, personal things, into a creek.'

'What about worms on sandwiches?' Susan persisted.

The ribbon was almost dry and looked none the worse, the slippers packed with paper by Anne still retained their shape, the books, Catty thought, might even pass Miss Shipp if she ironed each page, and the album only apeared to be defaced on its cover. She told Belinda that she would put a chintz face over the album, and Belinda looked cherubic and said she would forgive Susan.

The forgiveness was just too much. Catty looked shrewdly at the cherub face and decided there might be two sides to this.

'These worms . . .' she said.

'I opened up my lunch and I thought that sandwich looks different, so I parted it and it was worms.' This was Susan.

'Dead or squirming?' Ann Mary asked again.

'Quiet, Ann Mary. Belinda, did you do such a terrible thing?'

Belinda looked defiant. 'Susan took all my worms from my school plot. Worms are the Gardener's Help. We have that in Botany. She wanted her own plot to get First Prize.'

'They're having a contest, Sister Pussycat,' explained Anne.

'The Fifth Grade,' patronized Dorothea.

'So you went and took them back again, Belinda?'

'No, they'd all gone into her plot by that,' said Belinda angrily, 'she'll get First Prize for sure.'

'So?' prompted Catty.

'So I thought if she wants worms she can jolly well have worms. So I got some.'

'Where did you get them?'

'Up here.'

'From our own Sky House garden?' They had a little plot of sorts outside the door.

'No, Mr. Fitzsimmons's.'

Mr. Fitz was the Camp Universe gardener. Catty had a fair idea as to where Belinda had gone for her worms, for

Mr. Fitz recently had expended all his attention, as well as his under gardener's labour, on a new bed. Delivery had been taken of an expensive seed. Had Belinda's worm theft been Before Sowing or After Sowing? Catty dared not think of that just now.

'Then, Belinda?'

Belinda put on her cherubic look. 'I gave them to her, Sister Pussycat.'

'In a sandwich?'

'Well—'

'A sandwich?'

'Yes.'

'With butter?' asked Ann Mary.

'Dorothea, take Ann Mary outside.'

'But, Sister Pussycat—' protested Dorothea, who was enjoying herself.

'Outside. In fact everybody outside except Susan and Belinda.' As she gave the order, Catty felt a throb in her foot.

'Would you have let Susan eat that sandwich, Belinda?' she asked when they were alone.

'I knew she wouldn't because she always opens up her sandwich first.'

'But would you have let her?'

Belinda hung her head.

The foot was throbbing again. Catty changed its position and it eased a little. Her head ached and she felt muzzy. She longed to be wise and admonish both girls in an intelligent, constructive way, but she found she could not think.

'Go outside now,' she said. 'I'll have more to say later.'

As soon as they went she hobbled to her room and laid down. She put a pillow under the foot and it helped considerably. Five minutes, she thought, and I'll be all right. But she was denied even those five minutes.

Dorothea came to her door and called importantly, 'Mr. Fitz is here and he's mad as hell.' She was definitely

49

enjoying herself.

'Don't speak like that, Dorothea. Bring him in and give him a chair. Tell him I'll be out presently. And all of you go for a walk. I want no one listening at the door.'

'Oh,' said the deflated second eldest.

Catty got up and at once a flash of pain encompassed her. She waited until it throbbed away, then forced on a slipper and went out.

Mr. Fitzsimmons sat on the chair, and undeniably, Catty saw, he was as mad as h— Well, he was an extremely annoyed man.

'Bobby-dazzler,' he greeted Catty, 'the Flower of the Year! The half pound of seed cost me—'

'What is Bobby-dazzler, Mr. Fitzsimmons?'

'A petunia, of course. I thought everybody knew that.'

'I see. And this Flower of the Year?'

'An annual award. A marigold got it last time. Mind you, I thought the Empire Stock would get it. But I did agree with Bobby-dazzler this year, and that's why—'

'Tell me about your flower bed,' prompted Catty. The throb was starting again. She had to hurry this up.

'Well, I put Bobby-dazzler in the bed. You might remember, Sister, that I showed you how I'd prepared the bed.'

'Yes. The plot looked lovely. So' . . . unhappily . . . 'the seed was in.'

'Yes, the Bobby-dazzler. And what happens when I come the next morning? It's all dug up!'

Catty wondered for a cowardly minute if she could put the blame on an animal . . . or even a boy. It was unfair, she knew, but the foot was hurting quite badly, and all she wanted to do was get rid of Mr. Fitzsimmons.

'Dug up by a *girl*,' said Mr. Fitz. 'Left her footprint. You could tell straight away.'

'Can you?' asked Catty helplessly.

'Yes, Sister.'

'But couldn't . . . I mean feet are feet.' Not *her* foot, it must have cornered all the pain in the world.

'The soles,' said Mr. Fitz triumphantly. 'Different, Sister. The boys' soles have a rubber pattern. The girls' soles are in a composite material.'

'I believe you,' said Catty wearily. 'I'll see that the girl is reprimanded. I'll see that you're recompensed. Please, Mr. Fitz, please go.'

He went at last, a little placated at having had his say but still indignant. Yet still Catty could not lie down, for the girls returned, and Dorothea said eagerly, 'Dinner is on. The boys are there. You did say, Sister Pussycat, that we might all eat together.'

'After a disgusting, shameful, outrageous affair like this?' At least Catty could use that, for she never had felt less like altering a system in all her life.

Dorothea's face fell, and Catty felt sorry for the child . . . but sorrier for herself.

'We'll go across for dinner,' she announced.

'But the boys haven't left yet,' said Anne, mindful of their deprivation.

But they will, Catty knew, by the time I get there, all you children with me.

'Did you tread on a nail, Sister Pussycat?' asked Ann with concern as they went slowly across the lawn.

'Or sharp glass?'

'Or old tin?'

'Or—'

'Girls, stop!' Catty knew her voice was little short of shrill. She got the wards into the dining-room, superintended their collection of their plates, their return of their plates, marched them back again, sat with them over their homework, checked that they bathed and 'went'. Then she limped exhaustedly to her own room and fell on to the bed.

After a while she recovered sufficiently to put a pillow under the foot, and once again it eased. Reluctant to start it off again, she just lay there still in her clothes. It would be better in the morning, she thought hopefully. If she didn't disturb it she might go to sleep, and when she woke up . . .

She did not wake up, for she did not lose consciousness, but she must have drifted a little, for the first flash of pain caught her so sharply she had to sit up to stop crying out.

She took off the bandage and examined the wound as much as she could, but it was difficult on the sole of the foot.

She had had her T.T. – tetanus toxoid – but the promptness with which the pain had encompassed her she found rather alarming. What if there had been a mistake in the toxin? Things like that could happen. She found herself thinking of what she had been told about tetanus, that the outlook is influenced by the length of time which elapses between the wound and the symptoms. Recovery chances were considerably less when infection struck promptly. Oh, why was she going on like this?

But it's hard to be reasonable in the a.m. hours. Did she feel giddy? Did she want to yawn? Was there a stiffness in her throat muscles? Had she—

Exhausted, she fell back again on to the bed, and this time she did sleep . . . to be awakened by Anne saying apologetically that the boys were finished breakfast and they had better get across, because it was school, and they had their sandwiches to cut. Yes, worm sandwiches, thought Catty dully. She saw Anne looking at her crushed clothes.

'Dear, I don't feel well. Take the girls across and tell Mrs. Chester.'

'It would be better to ring Doctor David, Sister Pussycat.'

'No. No, not him.'

'There's no other doctor.'

'Mrs. Chester will know.'

'She doesn't, though. She sends for Doctor David for everything.'

... Yes, I know, thought Catty weakly, remembering miserably what Mrs. Chester had said. 'I fear I've been worrying our doctor far too much.' Catty recalled thinking it would only be a worry *when it was a girl*.

'Mrs. Chester, Anne,' she said, and lay back again.

Of course it was no use arguing with that good lady when she came. Mrs. Chester took one look at her and fled to the phone. Lying still and wretched, Catty asked honestly of herself: Would I sooner slip out of life or be treated by this man? Life was precious, of course, but on the other hand she would have given anything not to be lying helpless here waiting for the honorary medical adviser to Camp Universe to come through the door, look down on her and say haughtily: 'Well, Sister Quentin?'

'Well, Sister Quentin?'

The only difference was that instead of standing haughtily he sat down on the bed ... though haughtily ... so as to be closer to the wound.

'My foot,' she managed.

'Presumably.' He took up the foot and she flinched

'I've had my T.T.,' she told him, trying to be professional.

He did not appear to hear it, he kept examining, probing. Then after a long time, or it seemed a long time, he looked up and said: 'Thought you had tetanus, eh?' He actually and hatefully grinned.

'I knew I hadn't,' coldly.

'*In the small hours?*' he taunted. 'I've no doubt you were checking every known symptom.'

She did not answer, but she knew her burning cheeks answered him. He laughed ... hatefully ... again.

'Where did you cop this?'

'In the creek.'

'How in Betsy were you in the creek?'

'I was rescuing Belinda's things.'

'In the creek.'

'I told you,' she said.

'But you didn't tell enough. How did they get there?'

53

'Susan threw them. Oh, it wasn't her fault, at least' . . . at a look in his face . . . 'not entirely.'

'No?'

'No, you see Susan was upset about the worms. So' . . . miserably as she remembered Mr. Fitzsimmons . . . 'was the gardener. All those Bobby-dazzlers. – Doctor Jasper, what are you doing?'

For David Jasper seemed to be preparing a needle, looking at her intentionally as he did so.

'You're so little short of delirious,' he said, 'it doesn't matter.'

'I'm not delirious. Belinda made a worm sandwich and put it in Susan's lunch. They'd been feuding.'

'To say the least,' he inserted. 'What about the gardener?'

'She . . . Belinda . . . dug them out of his prize bed. Bobby-dazzlers. That' – hurriedly, seeing another intentional look – 'is the name of the particular petunia strain.'

'I think,' he said, 'I'm seeing light. Susan, incensed, comes home, takes up Belinda's belongings and throws them in the creek. You run down to rescue them and either step on a nail, some glass—'

'Or a tin,' said Catty, borrowing from the girls.

'Well, the thing to do is to give you a boost, even though you've had your T.T., or so you say.'

'I have. Was that needle a boost all the time?'

'What did you think it was? Something to quieten you down while I sent for a straitjacket?' He was pushing up her sleeve, swabbing her arm, injecting her quickly and expertly.

'Next,' he said, 'we'll probe the foot. I'll freeze it first, and' . . . a pause . . . 'be as gentle as I can.'

'Thank you,' she said.

She felt the probe, but only distantly, almost as if he was picking at the skin.

'You see,' he said once, looking up, 'I can be gentle.'

'Even to a female?'

'That was unnecessary. I'm a doctor, and to a doctor a patient, whatever sex, is a very precious person.'

'In what way precious?'

'It's glass,' he said, ignoring her. 'One piece is embedded in such a way that it would cause considerable distress.'

'Can it be removed from this precious patient?'

'It's out now.' He had pricked again and removed something, still painlessly. 'Only you'll have to lie up a while. However, there are lots of things you can do, I expect. Case histories, for instance, parent – if any – approach.'

'Belinda's album. I promised to re-cover it.' At once Catty wished she had not spoken, for his face darkened. He would, she thought, be a very stern man . . . especially with girls.

'The album that went into the drink?'

'Yes.'

'What do you intend doing about that?'

'I'm covering it. I said so.' She added, foolishly she knew, 'in chintz.'

'What are you doing about the miscreants?' he corrected icily. 'Like Ann Mary and the sugar sandwich, are you going to pat their heads and say "Good girls"?'

'I didn't reward Ann Mary.'

'Well, you didn't punish her.'

'I didn't pat her head.'

'Nor pat her anywhere else.'

'If you're implying that these children should be—'

'I said pat, not thrash, flog, apply with a cat-o'-nine-tails. How you women flare!'

'My girls will be dealt with.'

'By you?'

'Who else?'

'By me, Sister. You're incapable of dealing with them now while you're laid up like this.'

'Doctor Jasper, I will not have my children maltreated!'

'My *precious* patient,' he said witheringly, 'you will lie where you are and leave this to me. For if you dare to move, and I mean this, you'll be removed to Penrith Hospital. Now I've wasted too much time on one case. I'll call in again tonight, make sure there's no infection.'

'The girls—'

'Listen for their screams,' he advised cruelly, and he strode out.

Though she knew she was being ridiculous, Catty did listen for screams. For cries at least. And cries she heard. But they were from all the girls, not just Belinda and Susan. There were more soft, distressed cries as they came tiptoeing in.

'Oh, Sister Pussycat, you're sick!'

'Oh, Sister Pussycat, don't leave us.'

'We'll be good, Sister Pussycat.'

'Darling Sister Pussycat!'

'Sister Pussycat, if we don't keep quiet they might have to take you away.'

But worst punishment of all was Belinda's and Susan's punishment. They were pale and strained and they stayed behind after the others left to whisper, 'Don't die, Sister Pussycat, we'll never be bad like that again.'

What had he said to them? It didn't sound, Catty decided, like approved child psychology, but, and she had to admit it, it had results.

She re-covered the album. She straightened the leaves of the library books. She mended. She read case histories. She talked with Mrs. Chester.

But all the while, and she was sharply conscious of it, sharply angry with herself for the consciousness, she was aware of the hours that would turn the day into night … when he, Doctor David Jasper, would attend his 'precious' patient again.

He came in after the children were bedded that evening.

'A heavy stint,' he said, and sat down and closed his

eyes for a few minutes. As when he smiled, when he closed his eyes he lost that long look. He seemed almost boyish.

Then he opened the eyes and asked, 'How is it, Sister Pussycat?'

She was so startled at his address that the colour leapt up in her face, and he laughed lightly and said, 'If you react like that to a child's name for you, how would you react to a – lover's?'

'I have no lover,' she said stiffly.

'I didn't ask you that, I asked how would you react to "Darling", to "Beloved", to— But now you've told me you have no lover, so you can't answer, of course. – Unless you have memories.' Another light laugh.

'Oh, I have memories.' She was not aware of the bitterness in her voice. Just before he had come she had been going through a small bag she had had Anne fetch in for her, and from it she had withdrawn a photograph wallet of two small people – Gaby and Georgie. Once again she had known the pain of loss, and then an anger against Lilla who had inflicted the loss.

'So you have memories,' he said, putting his own construction on her words.

'My foot feels considerably better,' she broke in.

'In other words,' he grinned, 'keep to business. Yes, it does look improved, Sister Quentin, but you're still to lie up.'

'If it's better—' she started to protest.

'In a private citizen's world,' he came in blandly, 'a person may choose for himself whether he obeys his doctor, or tells him to go to damnation. But here you're not a private citizen, not in Camp Universe, so you do as you're told.'

'And think the damnation?' she dared.

'I have no doubt that that's what you're thinking now, but the order still stands. Do you understand?'

'I would be a fool not to understand a member of the Board.'

'You would,' he agreed amiably. 'Same time tomorrow night. Leg up, Sister Quentin.' He went out.

She caught up with the darning. She studied Mr. Chester's ward backgrounds. She tried to establish some of their medical facts.

The children were sweet, so sweet that she found herself clenching her hands. I won't love them back, I won't allow it; remember Gaby and Georgie, remember the pain. Don't let it happen again, because unmistakably it has happened to them. *They love me.*

Bit by bit she pieced together the fabric of their love. Most of the threads *were* love, love unclaimed that they carried around in their small eager hearts, waiting to use it up. They needed someone to love. They had to have someone. The other house-mothers had cast their offerings aside. Catty thought she had, too, but perhaps she had done it in a gentler way and they hadn't understood. Either that or they were very determined. They gave her all their love.

On the doctor's third visit she had the small bag out again, the wallet of her children. As he came in she put it down hurriedly. She hadn't thought he noticed, but he said, quite sharply, 'Who was that?'

'Just someone to do with me. Why?'

'Nothing.' But instead of sitting down he went to the window and looked out for a while. Then he turned back and said tersely, 'You can get up tomorrow.'

'Thank you.' She added, 'You needn't sound so short about it. Do you prefer me immobile?'

'At least then you're not in trouble.' He still sounded absent. 'What was that photograph?' he asked.

'My children. I've been married.' She said it flippantly, unprepared for his sudden tight grasp on her wrist.

'I'm sorry,' he said at once, 'I must have sounded nosey.' He let her go.

'You did.'

'Then accept my apologies. I have news for you. The Board have agreed to your purchase of swimsuits for the

58

girls. Do you want to do it by mail or go down and make a selection?'

'Sydney is rather a distance just for swimsuits,' she regretted, 'yet mail ordering doesn't always provide the right colour.'

'The right colour for learning to swim?' he disbelieved.

'Certainly. It has to be bright so you can't lose sight of them, but on the other hand how could I teach Marion, for instance, who had brilliant red hair, in a shocking pink suit?'

He said he was out of his depth, but told her that either Penrith or Parramatta, closer than Sydney to Emu Heights, had excellent stores.

'I'll take you down tomorrow.'

'Can Dorothea have a day off school and come, too?'

'Why?'

'She's going on for fifteen. At fifteen you don't just get a swimsuit flung at you and told "This is it".'

'Is that how you intend to treat the other fourteen?'

'Of course not, but you see . . . well, what I mean . . .'

'I don't see. I don't know what you mean. Anne, I believe, is older than Dorothea.'

'But different.'

'I still don't follow. However, it appears you want Dorothea with you. Probably the prospect of a long drive with me makes you feel you must have a girl.'

'For goodness' sake!' broke in Catty, irritated.

He had the grace to grin. 'It seems I'm on the wrong track.'

'You are.'

'Then Dorothea's not being taken along just to relieve the tension?'

'She's being taken along . . . that is, I hope she is . . . to choose her own bathers. Red, blue, pink, one-piece—'

'No bikinis,' he stipulated.

Catty did not argue; she had no intention . . . then . . . of letting Dorothea have her heart's desire, not until she had earned it, until she could swim.

'I'll have a form made out for you,' he told her. 'You just hand it to the saleslady and sign the docket. I have an easy day tomorrow. I'll call for you . . . and Dorothea . . . at eleven.'

He got up and nodded to her, his eyes as he did so resting briefly on the photograph wallet she had turned face down. For a moment there was a conflicting look on his own face.

Then: 'Goodnight, Sister Quentin,' he said.

He was there right on time. Catty had the feeling that this man always would be on time, always would do what he said he would do. In short, the perfectionist, she said sneeringly to herself.

She was aware that he was watching her with amusement as she put Dorothea into the middle seat, and only that that was where a young person should travel (and where she herself withdrew from travelling) she would have brazened it out just to have challenged that 'I told you' look on his face.

As it was she pretended not to hear that soft bantering laugh.

They set off down the valley, passing the citrus groves, the pea fields and pumpkin acres. A mile of rich flats chequered in vegetable patches and herb plots, then the river stretched out, a lovely sweep of singing green, uncoiling like a ribbon, with cobblestones on either side, or sometimes a span of creamy sand, or willow, or bramble and sloe with birds darting in and out.

They crossed the river by a silver bridge, then they were in Penrith, a country town in the old style, one long, shop-bordered main street.

David Jasper parked the car and suggested an early lunch. Catty was inclined to say no, that they could do their shopping and get back to the Camp. But Dorothea's eager face stopped her. Again she heard the doctor's faint laugh.

'It can't be a pub,' he said quietly to Catty, nodding at Dorothea, 'will a tea shop do?'

'Of course,' she said severely.

They found a pleasant one, and Doctor Jasper let Dorothea choose all the things teenagers like to choose. Just, he smiled to Catty, this once.

'When I think of school milk and sandwiches!' revelled Dorothea, tucking into sausage rolls, an ice-cream and a coke.

'The way you're gobbling,' warned David, 'you won't be fitting into a swimsuit, young woman, you'll need two sheets hemmed together.'

Dorothea was put off her meal for one moment. 'Am I getting fat? I mean, in a bik—'

Catty came in quickly, 'Frances, Dorothea? Do you think blue or green?' She was uncomfortably aware that she could be starting something and was annoyed with herself that she had not let Dorothea finish what she had to say about the bikini and have David Jasper say his piece at once. Too late now. She put down her cup and said primly, 'Thank you, it was a nice meal.'

'Fab,' Dorothea agreed.

'Now, you two young women,' said David when they were out on the street again, 'it's all yours. I have a few things to do up at Penrith Hospital, then I'll meet you at the car.'

'You're not coming in to choose, too, Doctor David?' asked Dorothea.

'Not on your life,' he assured her.

'If it were boys, Dorothea—' Catty could not stop herself saying that.

'There would be no need to choose,' David Jasper said. 'Just an order would do. Three dozen trunks. – One hour, not a minute more.' He strode off.

The women's wear shop for which she had the chit was large, modern and comprehensive. Catty could see she would get everything here she could have got in Sydney.

The saleslady was helpful and interested, and, supplied with ages and measurements, brought out each suit. Catty wanted them individual. She knew herself from her own childhood how important this was, yet how infrequently it had happened. Ideas were different now, she thought thankfully.

She also wanted bright colours, colours that accosted the eye. She turned down water blues and pool greens. If a child got into difficulties the colours must jump out at her.

At length they had finished all but Dorothea's. The saleslady brought forward a trim scarlet one-piece that she said should suit the older girl.

'Oh, no, Sister Pussycat, you promised me—'

'I didn't really, darling, I said—'

'But, Sister Pussycat, all the bigger girls, I mean *all* of them, they wear—'

'Not Anne, and she's senior to you.'

'But Anne's different, Anne is – well, she's Anne.'

'Dorothea, you're still very girlish, and I hardly think—'

'Sister Pussycat, I don't want this one. You know what I want.'

'You're very young, Dorothea, I mean ... Oh, Dorothea!' For tears had sprung into the girl's eager eyes.

If Dorothea had argued, Catty might have stood firm, persuaded her to accept the one-piece at least until she could swim, as they had agreed. But Dorothea just stood there with big, tear-wet eyes.

And suddenly it was years ago, and Catty was Catty in the days before Mother and Roger, Catty was begging for something and saying, 'If you'll only let me I'll never ask for anything any more.'

The little girl Catty had *not* got it ... what had it been, the woman Catty now tried, unsuccessfully, to recall ... *but Dorothea would.*

The saleslady was catching Catty's eye. She was a sympathetic person.

'Really more of a two-piecer,' she whispered, 'quite suitable for the immature deb figure.'

'She really does want it.'

'They all do,' the saleslady assured her. 'Can I show it to her?'

Catty nodded.

As a bikini, it was more of a one-piece suit with a midriff, but Dorothea was in raptures.

'Wrap it up,' said Catty quickly, telling herself that a senior should have something different, remembering guiltily how she had changed the conversation at lunch almost as though she had known this was going to happen. Hoping David Jasper had not noticed.

He was waiting at the car when they had finished, and once more they took the climbing road to the Camp.

Dorothea still sat between them, but she might just as well have not been there at all. Her eyes were starry. Catty knew she did not hear a word. David came to this conclusion, too, after he asked her several questions and she did not reply.

'What happened in there?' he laughed, and Catty bit her lip. What a web to weave! she despaired.

However, with ordinary good luck the web would not be discovered. She hardly thought a busy man like Doctor Jasper would be present at any swimming lessons . . . any *girls'* swimming lessons.

When he began talking over Dorothea's head, in the interest of what he had to say she forgot any misgivings. He told her again about the fire that had destroyed the medical records, and how he was trying to establish what protections the children had had.

'And it's no use you saying in a shocked voice "Of course they've had this, have had that", because it could be that they haven't.'

'How about their parents?'

'Usually one parent, and he or she won't know, or will think so, or think not. As for the girls . . . well, who wants a needle if a glib "I've had one already, Doctor" will do the trick?'

'Then start again.'

'Not advised, unless you *really* don't know.'

'Well, you don't know.'

'Perhaps. That's where you can help, Sister Quentin. Probe them. Get at them. You see, in a couple of instances I hesitate to afford a protection that might be already afforded. It's simply not advisable. I needn't go into medical facts. I'll do it, of course, if I must, but if you can help—'

She promised to, for she saw the urgency of wasting no time just as he saw it. Thank goodness, she said aloud, they were in a healthy place where the girls should establish a fair amount of immunity.

He agreed, adding, 'Apart from a safety measure, your swimming regime will help that health standard. That was a contributing reason when I spoke to the Board about commencing lessons.'

'Yes,' she said a little faintly, the web beginning to weave again.

But once in Sky House, and the children clambering around her, calling excitedly over their suits, she put her doubts aside. A little girl called Catriona, she smiled to herself, was getting what she had yearned for after many years. — What had it been? she wondered again.

Catty *knew* she got it in the joy in Dorothea's eyes.

CHAPTER FOUR

As spring weather often does, the temperature suddenly dropped, winter was brought out of mothballs again and any thought of beginning a swimming project was put aside for balmier days.

The children were disappointed yet by no means anxious to brave the windswept pool. As for Catty, nothing could have pleased her more. By the time she did begin lessons, she thought, no one ... meaning outsiders, for she sincerely hoped the children would retain their present enthusiasm ... would be interested any longer. Dorothea's bikini would be noticed no more than the other fourteen bathing suits.

She concentrated in the meantime on trying to unearth medical facts from her wards. She knew that David Jasper would not rely on the word of a child ... what had he said they would glibly tell him when he mentioned needles: 'I've had one already, Doctor' ... and she rather suspected he would not rely on parents, either, not that meticulous man. But he had asked her to collect data, and she tried.

It was just as he had said.

'Oh, I had that needle.'

'Yes, and that one, too.'

Nora even boasted that she had had every needle in the world.

When Catty reported this to David Jasper at one of their meetings, he said, 'I thought so. But thanks for trying. Immediately I want to concentrate on rubella.'

'German measles?'

'Yes. It's terribly important, Sister.'

'I know. But if the girls are evasive again—'

'This time I won't waste time on any inquiries. In fact I intend exposing all Sky House next week. There's

German measles down in the valley. We'll take the entire bunch down. By the way, *you've* had them, of course?'

'I think I would have.'

'No "thinking",' he said sternly. 'If you haven't, then you must have them. Rather late, perhaps, but better that than never. Then when you have your own daughter—'

'You surprise me. I thought you only considered a male population.'

'When you speak idiotically like that I do only consider it.' He paused. 'Try to find out about rubella.'

The children didn't know it. How could she expect them to? Several of them said it was a nice name and when was the girl coming here to Sky House? How old was rubella?

'It's a complaint, a sickness, not a name. In fact it's measles.'

'Oh, I've had them,' some of them said.

'German measles, not the other ones.'

'Mine were spotty ones,' called Marion. 'Here and here and here.'

'Then they were measles. German measles are different, they—' She decided they were too young to understand, so told them about Saturday's picnic instead.

In due course the picnic materialized, a good time was had by all, but not so good when fifteen of the fifteen went down with a mild fever, rash and a hundred-degree temperature. David Jasper was joyful at his success; the girls, too, were jubilant that they were to remain in the Camp for seven days and miss school, but Catty, after the first day, was exhausted.

Then a woman from the village turned up and proved a marvellous help.

'I can't thank Mrs. Chester enough for thinking of you,' Catty once said to Mrs. Parker.

Mrs. Parker said, 'Don't thank Mrs. Chester, thank Doctor Jasper.'

'Oh,' Catty said then.

The spots disappeared, there were no complications, and seeing spring still had not returned there was no thought of the pool.

So Catty decided to start on her sex intermingling. The best place to begin, she thought, would be the meal room.

That first dinner with boys and girls together was as bad as it could be. Only valiant hearts like Tony's and Catty's could have emerged still hoping. Or, said Tony in a moment of cowardice, only two fools.

The boys were seated when the girls were marched in, and instantly there arose boos, catcalls, pleas of Help! Wimmen! and the inevitable wolf-whistles.

'Quiet!' Tony Williams shouted.

The girls collected their meals at the hatch and sat at another table. In time, Tony and Catty had decided, they would all eat *en famille*. But this was a try-out.

What a try-out! Bang into Belinda's soup, splashing her all over though not scalding her to death as she loudly complained, landed a marble, skilfully and covertly impelled there by a catapult.

'The boy with the shanghai can forfeit the rest of his meal!' Tony called. He walked round his table, questioned a few suspects, but unearthed no weapon.

The catapult was not brought out again, but it was amazing how far and how accurately food could be flicked. Susan and Marion got it in their eyes and on their noses.

Then somehow or other, even with Tony and Catty watching, Susan's ponytail was dipped in gravy. Marita's thick brown curls seemed to change colour, which is not surprising with an application of custard.

All the time the noise kept up ... the catcalls, the Help! Wimmen! The wolf-whistles.

'Wow!' Tony said as they emerged.

But they didn't give up. The next night there was no sudden surprise, therefore fewer calls. There were also fewer flicks of food and not one curl encased in custard.

67

'We're getting somewhere,' Tony said.

By the end of the week you would have thought that both sexes had dined together all their Camp lives. Catty was quite disappointed when Tony informed her that visitors were expected for the week-end, this time a bus-load of reprimanded first offenders sent up by a concerned magistrate, so for three nights the combined meal would be dropped.

'We'll have it all to go through again,' Catty wailed.

'Somehow I don't think so. We may have a slight recurrence, but the novelty of the girls is definitely over. It was really that novelty that was causing all the noise.'

But if Catty considered that was noise, she retracted the thought upon the arrival on Friday evening of the town children, brought to Camp Universe for a country week-end. She saw at once why Tony had put aside integration. He would be fully occupied keeping peace.

For the 'permos', as they proudly called themselves, naturally resented the visitors, especially when they put on patronizing city airs. However, they got their own back when the newcomers were introduced to the farm, for many of the boys had never been nearer to an animal than outside the cage of a zoo. It was Tony's job to mingle the two sections of young citizens amicably, but more often, he had told Catty feelingly, he spent three days acting referee.

Catty heard the Camp Universe bus pant up the last steep incline and then release its load. Out they spilled, boys so totally different from the permanents that they could have come from another planet. The Universe boys were short back and sides, but the visitors (except the Police Boys' Club members, who, Tony reported, were barbered before they were permitted to come) had distinctly long locks. Their clothes, too, varied greatly from the shorts and shirts of the permanents. They all wore slacks with studded belts, and quite a few dangled chains swinging large pendants around their necks.

Catty heard: 'Gaw, smell the place!' and knew that any smell that was not fish and chips, dust and trade waste was not normal air to them.

They complained, when night fell, about the dark. 'Where's the blinking lights?' ... 'How can you see to think?'

Daylight the next morning, however, humbled them. 'It's big,' they said, looking wonderingly into the distance. They also looked as though it was too big for them and they'd like to go home.

Mud horrified them. Some, Tony declared, had never seen mud, good clean honest mud, in their lives.

But at the finish of the week-end they were always 'hooked', Tony also said. Well, most of them. There were invariably some whom it had been a waste of time and money bringing up to Universe, but the others, the ones with a question in their eyes and a backward look as they left on Sunday night, made it worthwhile.

On the Monday, Catty once more introduced the girls, and though there were a few guffaws it was nothing like the initial night.

Which determined Catty to make her next move.

Tony, consulted, was at first dubious. 'Why should they wait on the boys?' he asked.

'It's a girl's role in life.'

'Are you saying that with your tongue in your cheek, are you anti-feminist?'

'I'm saying it in all truth. The majority of these girls will marry and have homes. Even if they become career women they'll need to know how to do this.'

'The boys will lord it over them.'

'Only for as long as it remains a novelty, and if that's only for as long as the girls were novelties, it won't be any time.'

'I don't know, Catriona. It does seem imposing on them.'

'And what about the girls imposing on the boys when

the boys attend to the piggeries, the fowl runs, milk the cows.'

'You have a point there,' he admitted. 'Well, if you feel the girls won't object—'

'If they do, I'll drop it at once. I'll see how they feel tonight.'

There was no need for Catty to dress up her suggestion. As soon as the wards understood what she proposed, every one of the fifteen could not wait to start. It appeared, Catty smiled later to Tony, that the domestic trait was the most powerful trait in a girl.

'I think it might have been that apron and cap you bribed them with.'

'The enthusiasm came before the apron and cap so there was no bribery, not even any recommendation. As a matter of fact' ... Catty smiled ... 'they were so gratifyingly keen, I couldn't resist dressing them up as a reward.'

She had bought the material for the aprons and caps out of her own money. After the Board's generosity with the swimsuits, she felt it was not fair to ask from them so soon again. Also, the bikini was still not quite out of her conscience; she wanted as little to do with any requirements from Universe Board as she could. Finally, this was entirely her affair.

The aprons were a pretty pink with a white frill. The caps were white and very becoming.

Of course the boys commented loudly on the innovation, but it was obvious that they quite liked it. Soon their calls of 'Waitress, over here' ... 'Slave, bring me—' ... 'Servant, take this—' would not meet the applause from the ones who had not made the remark, and the uniforms would be as accepted as the girls were.

'We're getting there,' Tony beamed.

'No, we're *there*,' Catty triumphed.

Poor Catty!

The next Saturday was visiting day. On visiting week-ends no outside sectors were brought in.

Catty was looking forward to meeting the parents, or as many parents as her girls could muster. Apart from trying to establish something of their home environment, she intended learning as much as she could extract from them of their child's medical background.

She learned a little of the environment even before they came.

For instance, Deborah, thirteen, whose abandoned mother had had to relinquish four of her seven because she could not keep them, could not wait for visiting day. A good relationship there.

On the other hand, Adrienne, twelve, did not look forward to her father. When her mother had left the family of four boys and a girl, and a girl had seemed too much for the worried father and had been boarded out, she had resented her exclusion, even though it had been explained to her as only for now, not later, and she refused to be elated by his visit. Poor Mr. Travis, Catty thought, I must tell him that it's only her vulnerable age and that it will all work out.

Nora, the reputed problem girl with whom Catty had had no problem, was not even slightly interested. She hoped neither of her parents came.

Mardi, their 'on loan' child, whose mother and father had suffered a car accident, was waiting eagerly for the visit of an adoring aunt to tell her how they were getting on. She was one of the lucky ones.

So was Heather, the little brown one, whom the Aboriginal Welfare Board indulged, Catty sometimes thought, enough for two girls. Heather told Catty someone would bring along chocolates and books for her.

Ann Mary's grandmother, whom it appeared was not dead after all ... 'That was another grandmother' ... and whom Catty was 'zackly like, so Ann Mary frequently said, was anticipated with joy. Susan, too, did not seem put out by the prospect of a relation.

But Anne, rising fifteen ...

71

'I hate visiting day,' Anne said.

Catty was pleased it was a fine morning, and that the new Bobby-dazzlers had sprung up nicely so that Mr. Fitz did not mind her taking flowers for the tables from his other beds.

The two o'clock bus from Penrith brought up the first contingent of parents. Some for the boys, some for the girls. She watched as some of her wards ran with open arms and some just sidled across. After the greetings were over, she joined the groups, talked a while, then finally edged in her medical inquiries.

From Mardi's aunt she learned that Mardi would most certainly have been given everything. Adrienne's father, too, a quiet, concerned little man, had said he had always been careful over health.

'Would you know if Adrienne as a baby had her triple antigen?' At the man's confused look, she explained, 'Diphtheria, tetanus, whooping cough. Also, what about polio, Mr. Travis?'

He seemed to know, and he gave a good answer, though Catty still felt sure that Doctor Jasper would take no risk.

She was a little startled at Ann Mary's grandmother, who was very old, and who looked . . . naturally . . . very pleased when Ann Mary said: 'See, I said you had the same face, Sister Pussycat.'

Anne's mother had arrived, but in a flashy car driven by a flashy man, who, when Catty went across and invited him in said: 'No, I'll wait for Junie. If you feel like a rest from the brats y'r welcome to sit here, too. In fact, Nurse' . . . an estimating look up and down Catty . . . 'y'r very welcome, though,' with a meaning laugh, 'I don't know what Her Ladyship would say.

Her Ladyship was awful. Catty knew it was awful of her to register that impression, but still she registered awful. It was not her clothes, which were quite good, it was the cheap impression of them. She looked tawdry. Even if she had worn mink she would have looked tawdry. Catty's heart went out to Anne.

'How do you get on with the Duchess?' Anne's mother asked. 'For I can tell you, I don't. It's not natural, the way she never comes to me. You wouldn't think we were mother and daughter.'

'No,' said Catty. She asked Anne's mother if she could persuade her friend to come inside for tea.

'Harry?' A laugh. 'Now, if you had a bar . . .'

'But *you* will come, won't you?'

'No. Harry only brought me up on condition that I didn't stop.'

'I'd particularly like you to come. There's something I want you to see.'

'I really don't think so, love. How long will it take?'

'Not long.'

'Then I'll have a word with Harry.'

While she went over to the car, Catty collected her girls and dressed them in their aprons and caps. By the time Anne's mother returned all the parents were seated and the 'maids' were walking around, very conscious of themselves, carefully balancing their trays of tea and cake.

They made a charming little scene, Catty thought . . . even Cooky came to the hatch to smile. Several of the parents beckoned Catty across to the table to compliment her on the idea, and those who didn't at least seemed content to be waited on by daughters in pink.

All but one parent. Anne's parent.

'What's this?' she said loudly, and sensing what was to come, Catty managed to get her outside.

'A fine thing,' she said, 'making domestics of them!'

'It wasn't the idea. You have it wrongly.'

'You put a girl in a cap and apron and have her wait on table, then tell me I have it wrongly? A servant, that's what you're making of her!'

'It's not like that. It was meant only for training.'

'Training to be a drudge!'

'It was fun. They all love it.'

73

'Well, I don't love it. I don't even like it. I have half a mind to take Anne away.'

Someone had joined them. Catty did not know whom it was until David Jasper said coldly, 'Please have no half mind about that, madam, take the girl away.'

Anne's mother was looking the doctor up and down, speculating about him. She must have decided he was no Harry, for she did not alter her antagonistic expression.

'I think I will.'

'Don't think,' he advised.

'The Government pays this place for these girls.'

'It will also pay you when you take Anne home.'

'I've a mind to. Domestic, indeed!' she sniffed.

'Shall I tell Anne to go and pack her bag?'

'Waiting on table, fetching for people!'

'Sister Quentin, kindly remove Anne to the dormitory and superintend her while she collects her things.'

Catty stood aghast ... so, also, did Anne, who, sensing what was going on, had come across.

'Sister Pussycat, I can't ... I can't ...' she whispered in agony.

'Sister Pussycat!' sneered Anne's mother.

'Sister Quentin, I gave you an order. If you will wait five minutes, madam—'

Catty said dully, 'Come along, Anne.'

'Wait!' Anne's mother said sharply. When they did so, she said, much less sharply, in fact almost in a slow whine, 'It's hard for me. Her father left me when she was a baby. The struggle I've had, no one knows.'

'We have a fair idea here at Camp Universe. No doubt you were very lonely. No doubt you are now. It will be company for you with your daughter home.'

'No,' said Anne's mother sharply again, 'no!'

'You just said she was to leave.'

'I was speaking out of turn. I'm not the best lately. My nerves ... you know all about that, Doctor,' a coy look.

'Yes, I know,' David Jasper said. 'Will you tell your friend you're waiting for Anne, he seems a little impatient.' That was an understatement. Harry had a fat finger on the horn.

'He has to get back. You know these big businessmen. If it's all the same to you . . .' She began edging away.

'What's all the same? What do you mean?' David said politely but firmly.

'Anne. I can't take her. I mean how can I in my position?' Anne's mother began to cry.

Catty wanted to call out, 'Then leave her . . . *leave* her,' but David Jasper repeated: 'You just said she was to go.'

'I was angry about that business.' A nod to the dining-room. 'No daughter of mine will ever be—'

'Sister Quentin, I believe I told you to take Anne across to get her bag.'

'Of course' . . . Anne's mother again . . . 'if Anne is excused domestic duty—'

'Sister Quentin!' The sharpness in David's voice startled Catty into action. Taking Anne's hand, she stepped out.

But only one step.

'Wait,' said Anne's mother. Then: 'I'll go through this another time.'

'Now.'

'I have to go. Harry—'

'Go with Anne or without Anne?'

'I want to take her, but you know how hard it is—'

'You're leaving her at Camp Universe?'

'Well – well, yes.'

'To go on as she's going now?'

'Well, you know how it is.'

'*Are* you?'

'. . . Yes.'

'Good afternoon, madam.' David Jasper turned and said deliberately, 'There are visitors without afternoon tea, Anne.'

'Yes, Doctor David.' Anne, without a look at her mother, hurried inside.

75

But Catty? Catty went behind a pillar holding up the porch and cried. Cried till someone coming deliberately beside her to hide her from any curious eyes said, 'It's all right, they've left. She's still yours.'

I don't want her, was what she should have said, for she is love, and I don't want love, any sort of love, not ever any more.

She did not say it. She just stood in the protection of his large shadow. After a while she was calm again.

When the parents had gone, David Jasper sauntered across to Sky House.

Catty had been trying to make out a list of her medical gleanings for him and when he entered, she handed him the paper.

'Not so comprehensive as I wanted,' she regretted. 'How can parents be so vague?'

'It doesn't matter. I think I would still have doubly insured, anyway, even had I known. But thanks. Sister Pussycat.' – Sister Pussycat. Again he said it. She darted a quick glance at his face. It had an expression she could not categorize. She turned her own glance away.

'I did some probing of my own,' he offered. 'I should say that Mardi and Adrienne have been well safeguarded, probably a few others.' He looked down on her list. 'I see that this agrees with your gleanings.' He discussed other girls, then asked, 'Did you establish any environmental backgrounds?'

'Backgrounds establish themselves.' She stopped the beginnings of a sigh.

He knew she meant Anne, but he did not pursue that.

'Anyone else in particular?' he asked.

'Adrienne, for one. Her father is nice.'

'And at his wits' end,' agreed David. 'Four boys and a girl. He only placed her here thinking it was best.'

'It wasn't best.'

'Not in the way you're thinking, and yet in the name of

common sense the only move.'

Catty nodded.

They went through several other names, then because he was not mentioning Anne, and wanting to thank him for Anne, Catty mentioned her herself.

'How did you know?' she asked.

'Know?'

'That Anne's mother wouldn't take her home.'

'I knew.' He smiled lopsidedly. 'My only concern was that you would spoil it all. You were aching to wave a flag of surrender, weren't you, you longed to come to terms.'

'I was frightened she would remove Anne.'

David Jasper said contemptuously, 'Not her.'

A little silence fell between them. Catty hoped it emerged a grateful silence on her behalf.

The doctor broke it. He said, 'You've become involved with these children, haven't you?'

'Oh, no!' Her answer was so intense that it fairly cut into the room.

He turned narrowed eyes on her. 'It certainly seems so.' No answer. 'What is it?' he broke in after a tight kind of pause. If her voice had been sharp, his was rapier-keen. 'Don't you want to be involved?'

'I'm not.'

'Don't you want to be?' he persisted, and his persistence demanded an answer.

'No,' she said.

'Why?'

'Because – because there's no love left, not ever any more. Any sort of love.'

'I see.'

He gathered up the papers she had filled for him, thanked her gravely, then went to the door.

'The weather is changing,' he said non-committally, 'I think we're returning to spring.'

He nodded and went out.

The next morning it was not just spring it was spring

touching hands with summer. The sun was up before Sky House was, making a lacy pattern on Mr. Fitz's well-mown grass, and over the chequered green of it drifted a rain of wisteria blossoms in the tenderest purple. A lovely lovely day.

When Dorothea said eagerly that it was warm enough to swim, the other fourteen agreed. Catty should have felt satisfied over that, and she was, of course, though . . .

Oh, don't be foolish, she upbraided herself, one very moderate bikini. – Which you did not report, whispered a small voice.

It was Sunday, and after service in Horizon Hall a free day. Catty checked with Tony as to whether the boys would be swimming and if so what hour, then told her wards the pool was theirs between eleven and noon.

Previously she had decided to teach the girls to look after themselves in the water, not to worry about niceties of stroke and style. If any of them showed promise they could be taught from scratch again.

She let them hi-jink around for a while, then she jollied each in turn to try and touch her toes with her head down. After a few spluttering attempts they all succeeded in coming up smiling, and that was a first hurdle spanned. To go under and come up with a grin meant you had made friends with the water.

While she was assisting each in turn to dog-paddle across the shallow end by pretending they were pups after a stick, and lending them confidence by putting her hand under their chins, David Jasper sauntered across and stood watching. To her relief, and she felt sly and evasive over it, she stood in front of Dorothea, though Dorothea, who had taken enthusiastically to the water, was well under.

David watched a while, then strolled off.

'Time's up,' Catty said soon afterwards.

As the girls came out she towelled their arms, shoulders and legs vigorously, then wrapped them in their towels.

'More of me to do, Sister Pussycat,' giggled Dorothea,

still purring over her adult-sounding if not so much looking bikini, and Catty, about to toss a laughing rejoinder, was beaten to the response by a sound of disgust. At least had she had to describe it Catty would have said disgust, though how, unless one said the word, did one express disgust?

This was disgust, though, she felt sure of it, and she glanced at the woman who was passing by the pool.

'That's Mrs. Frances,' reported Dorothea. 'She's yu—'

'No,' Catty said. 'Now when I count three see who can be first back to the dormitory. One, two . . .' She raced off as well at three, for the wind was fresh. She was laughing and rosy with the rest of them when she got to Sky House, no thought at all about the woman who had walked by the pool, in fact no thought any longer about a bikini.

She was thinking about both within the hour.

'Here's Doctor David again,' called Mardi. 'He comes a lot more than he ever did with the older house-mothers. Why, Sister Pussycat?'

'Probably I don't know as much about children as they did, so he feels he should check me.' It would be more to do with the med. records, she thought, he would want to discuss them.

'You do *so* know about children!' they called lovingly, and Dorothea, bikini Dorothea, said adultly, 'I think he *likes* Sister Pussycat.'

She said it in such a way that even the smallest of them sensed that it was a different like from their like. Because they were females, and born with romance, they beamed at Catty.

'Oh, really,' she said helplessly, not knowing how to correct them.

At that moment the doctor entered, and because he faced Catty and not them, the children did not see the *lack* of liking in his face. In fact at that moment he obviously heartily *dis*liked her.

'Dismiss, girls,' she said at once. 'Doctor has something

79

to say to me.' Say to her? That must be the under-statement of the year, she thought ruefully; by the looks of him he wanted to snarl it.

He waited until the last child went out, then said briefly what he had come to say.

'We have a patroness, Mrs. Frances.'

'Oh, yes?' Mrs. Frances. Where had she heard that before?

'Mrs. Frances has the big red house farther up the hill. Perhaps you've noticed it.'

'Oh, I have. It's very beautiful.'

'It's her mountain house. She has also a town and sea-side house.'

'Nice for her.'

'Yes,' he said levelly, 'but not so nice now for us.'

'Why? Is she going away?'

'No, her patronage is.'

'To where?'

'I haven't asked her.'

'Then – then what is all this about?'

'About you. About Dorothea. About a set of swimmers that you said you didn't buy, but did.'

'By the "set of swimmers", as you modestly put it, I presume you mean a bikini.'

'You know what I mean,' he replied.

'And how does this Mrs. – er – Frances come in?' She remembered the name perfectly, but she made herself appear vague. 'Was it Frances or Franklin?'

He did not bother to answer that.

'She was passing the pool, to which quite a lot of her money went,' he said instead.

'You needn't go on with the disastrous story. I heard her grunt of disgust. It was her sight of Dorothea, wasn't it, Dorothea in rather old hat swimming things. I should say "set of swimmers".'

'Dorothea in a bikini you assured me you had not bought. Why did you do that?'

'I didn't – I mean I just didn't correct you.'

80

'Why?' he asked again.

'Because I didn't see anything wrong with it. I still don't. A girl rising fifteen.'

'I wasn't speaking about that, I was asking why you deliberately deceived me. Surely I could have been taken into your confidence if the need was that pressing, surely you could have come to me and said: "Look, it's important that this girl—" '

'And what good would it have done?' Catty paused. 'What' ... remembering back to a little girl who had asked and not received ... 'good does it ever do?'

He was looking at her sharply.

'Why should you ask that?'

'Because I was one, too,' she cried, 'and not even as well endowed as Dorothea. I was entirely unbelonging.'

There was a long silence. Had she dared look up she would have seen the strained corners of his mouth, seen that he was trying to find words to say. But when at last he did find them they were cool and taunting.

'Little Orphan Catriona,' he said. 'Tell me the rest of the sob-story.'

'You're hateful!'

'I am also' ... he said carelessly ... 'a fellow member. Yes, I, too, did not belong. That should provide us with quite a bond.'

'But it doesn't, does it? How could I have a bond with anyone so – so narrow as to object to a girl in a bi—'

He stopped her angrily. 'You little fool, you know it's not that. Had I my way all the kids would swim as they did in the very beginning of the universe, not as is laid down in Camp Universe.'

'Then—'

'It was your evasion, Sister Quentin.'

'I didn't mean it. I really didn't mean it,' she said sincerely. 'It just happened, that's all. Dorothea wanted the bikini, which incidentally is a very modest bikini, and suddenly I was a small girl wanting something desperately some fifteen years ago ... Oh, you wouldn't understand.'

'I understand,' he said quietly.

'So I let her, and then it was so easy not to tell you. I believed it would pass over. After all, it was a very small lie.'

He let her wait a long moment, and then he said almost gently, 'Yes, it was a small lie. But what on earth am I going to say to Mrs. Frances?'

'Is she really rich?'

'Filthy rich.'

'Has she really donated such a lot?'

'Such a lot we can't afford to do without her.'

'Then the answer is obvious. You must do without me.'

'*I* can't afford that,' he said. At least it sounded like that, but she couldn't be sure, for he was moving to the door.

'Doctor Jasper . . . David . . .'

He turned at the David, looking hard at her.

'Doctor Jasper, please let me help.'

His face stiffened, and he said, 'Haven't you done enough?'

'I'll speak to her.'

'Speak to no one, unless it's to tell your brats to be quiet long enough for Mrs. Frances to hear my pleas. What a rabble!'

'It's no louder than usual,' said Catty indignantly. 'Does the patroness also object to the voices of children?'

He did not answer that. He gave her a hard angry look and went out of Sky House.

There was no more about Mrs. Frances that day. Dinner with the boys was quite amicable, the girls were accepted now, their maids' uniforms an expected thing.

'Do you know a Mrs. Frances, Tony?' Catty asked.

'Yes,' he said.

'And what do you know?'

82

He said succinctly, 'Pots.'

'I see. Universe is anxious to retain her?'

'Naturally.'

'Is that good?'

'What she gives isn't bad,' grinned Tony.

'Does – does she dictate any principles?'

'Oh, no. David Jasper wouldn't stand for that.'

I think, thought Catty privately, he might.

The next night at dinner, which was the next time Catty met Tony, his day being more filled than hers with almost thirty young wards, a farm to watch, according to the nature of the sex more animal spirits to cope with, the house-father, or uncle – Catty had never learned which from Tony – had a beam from ear to ear.

'You look like the cat who got the cream,' she observed.

'Cream all right. We're getting a new gym. Oh, not the sort of gym you can share with folk dancing and ballet, but trapezes, training bicycles. Boys' things.'

'Who is the fairy godfather or mother?'

'Mother. Mrs. Frances.'

'You mean she's donating—'

'The boys. Strictly the boys. For some reason from now on everything must go to the boys. Sorry, Catriona.'

But Catty was relieved that Universe had not lost its rich patroness altogether. She wondered how fervent had been David Jasper's pleas.

He came over that afternoon for another chapter of Belinda, the amazing spacewoman. After he had finished the reading and dismissed the girls to the garden, he said to Catty, 'I suppose you heard the news.'

'The boys' new gym?'

'Yes.'

'I heard it, and I must say I was relieved that I hadn't lost you Mrs. Frances.'

'Oh, it wasn't easy. I had to talk very hard.'

'I'm sure you did.' In case he thought she was being facetious she hastened to add, 'I mean I'm sure you

83

exhausted yourself for Universe. Will you accept my thanks? Also' . . . as he nodded back . . . 'my apologies for the swimming business?'

'No,' he said of that, 'I won't.' As she stood deflated he went on, 'Because I'm sick of it. Talk about making a mountain out of a molehill . . .'

'You mean a gym out of a bikini,' she put in.

He looked back at her, and then, unexpectedly, he started to laugh.

After a moment Catty laughed, too.

The children, peeping in from the garden, joined irresistibly in the mirth.

'It's like a happy fam'bly,' Ann Mary beamed.

CHAPTER FIVE

THE new gym was started almost at once. Daily, little armies of workmen arrived at Camp Universe from Penrith or Emu Heights, and since most of them were young men, Catty kept her own brigade ... and Dorothea ... well away, in case Mrs. Frances, who continually superintended 'her' building, found something new to object to, even had a second mind about her generous offer.

All the girls could swim now. Even Ann Mary could manage a few puppy strokes without Catty's morale-building fingers under her chin. It gave Catty tremendous satisfaction to know that unless the circumstances were exceptional, these children might save themselves from drowning.

They were not considered to be up to the standard of Tony's young ruffians, who dive-bombed into the water, caught the legs of their friends and pulled them under, jumped on them, generally rough-housed each other, but, thought Catty, with vengeance in her against the opposite sex, give them time ...

She saw Bevan Bruce frequently, and at last, after so many invitations that she felt churlish not accepting, she agreed to go down for tea.

'I've a housekeeper, remember,' Bevan had reminded her when he had repeated the request.

She had burst out laughing, saying, 'Never the twain shall meet, segregation at Camp Universe. A chaperone at the Sunny Wonder Grove – with such precautions I must surely be in Grundy Acres.'

He laughed with her. 'You seemed to hesitate,' he stated. 'I knew it wasn't that, of course, but I had to reassure you, because ... well, because I want you there *very much*, Catriona,' he smiled boyishly.

She smiled warmly back at him. She liked him tremendously. She wondered what he would say if she told him she had hesitated because of Doctor Jasper. For in spite of the laughing note that had ended the bikini affair she was keenly aware of the latent disapproval in the medico that only needed the slightest misdemeanour on her part, or what he considered a misdemeanour, to bring that disapproval to the surface again.

And yet he was only *one* Board member, she told herself stoutly, and she had to have some relaxation. 'I'm looking forward to coming, Bevan,' she assured him.

Mrs. Mallard had a delicious afternoon tea waiting, and after the plain, if tasty, Universe fare, Catty found herself thoroughly enjoying herself.

When the tea was finished, she went for a more detailed tour of the grove than she had had before. Bevan had shown her all his citrus varieties, but he had not, he said in an offhanded manner that only emphasized his keenness, shown her his upstart row.

'Upstart, Bevan?'

'That feather and graft business, Catriona.'

'The bigger and better orange?'

'More than that. Cross-pollination between varieties as well as types. I keep a record of the seed parent, and . . . who knows? . . . one day I will raise a "citrange" or a "limequat".' He laughed. 'Seriously, though, it's a fascinating search to find the perfect fruit.'

Catty found all the citrus work fascinating. She watched keenly as Bevan attended a wounded tree. Surely Doctor Jasper did not afford his patients tenderer care. Where the bark had split on the trunk he bound it back with cotton strips, soaked previously, he told her, in melted grafting wax.

When they found another wounded tree, she begged to try her hand, and did the repair successfully. She looked proudly up from the completed job to see him looking steadily down at her.

'Catriona . . .' he said suddenly and softly.

She rose. The woman in her recognized that note in his

voice. 'Any more casualties, Bevan?' she asked briskly.

'Only this one,' he said honestly, and indicated himself.

'Where are the cotton strips and grafting wax?' She tried to laugh it away.

'I mean it, Catriona.'

'You're not to.'

'Oh, I know I'm bursting it out far too soon, but what can I do with all that competition?'

'Competition, Bevan?' she queried.

'Emu Heights fairly reeks with eager bachelors.'

'I haven't encountered them.'

'You've met three.'

'You' . . . she crinkled her eyes laughingly up at him . . . 'and—?'

'Tony Williams.'

'Ridiculous! And—?'

'David Jasper.' Bevan added ruefully, 'The most telling of all.'

Catty said incredulously, 'You must be quite crazy.'

'You don't like him?'

'I don't, as a matter of fact, but what I meant was he doesn't like me, he doesn't like any of my sex.'

'A man's man.' Bevan looked pleased for himself for that. 'Could be,' he mused, 'for I know I think the world of him.'

'Then you can think it.' An intentional pause . . . 'Bevan . . .'

'I know,' he forestalled, 'I did rush in. Forget it, Catriona.' But he still added with a pleading in his nice smile, 'For a while.'

As they walked back to the house he returned briefly and apologetically to the subject. 'I shouldn't have said that, I know, but somehow when a girl comes out from another country by herself, you kind of think there's a reason behind it, and I would never be one, when it was you, Catriona, to resent being a second thought.'

'You sound as though I came with a broken heart,' she

87

laughed. And then the laugh was dying in her. For I did, she knew, I did break my heart. She felt the sting of tears. Gaby. Georgie. Those dear little ones. My ones. Through the blur in her eyes she saw Bevan looking sympathetically at her and knew what he was thinking.

He took her up to Universe again, and there parked in front of Sky House, apparently waiting for her, was Doctor Jasper.

The two men spoke together for a while, then Bevan waved to Catty and went off, and David came into the common-room.

'Nice tea?' he asked.

'Lovely.'

'Nice afternoon?'

'Same answer,' she said tightly; she felt something was going to emerge.

'Nice man?'

'Oh, for goodness' sake!' she wheeled away, remembered that this person in a way was her employer, and came round again.

'That's better,' he said hatefully, 'never turn your back on a Board member.'

'What was it you wanted, Doctor Jasper?'

'Aren't we the diligent employee? Were you like this down in Sunny Wonder?'

'Bevan . . . Mr. Bruce is not a Board member. Did you want something?'

'Yes. I've received notice from the Department of Health today regarding the lost records. They've consulted duplicate files, and you'll be pleased to learn that the girls' immunization histories are all complete.'

'That's good,' she nodded.

'I was disregarding diphtheria and polio, surely nowhere these days has it not been made available.' He spread his hands. 'But I will admit I was wondering about tetanus.'

'As I was.' She dropped her animosity to smile in retrospect at herself.

'Yet particularly in this case.' He paused. 'Horses.'

'Horses?' So that was it. She had felt there was something he was going to break to her. She hoped she was not going pale, for that was what she felt. She had a dislike ... more than that, she was afraid ... of horses.

She forced herself to say casually: 'Horses?' as though they meant nothing to her. She tried to stop her mind from going back to that morning, years ago, not long after she had come to live with Mother on the small pleasant farm that Roger, after his father's death, had run for her. It was because of his farm duties and his frequent necessary absences from home that Mrs. Forbes, still grieving for a beloved husband, had brought Catriona to 'Meadows'.

'It had to be a girl,' she had told Catty lovingly, 'otherwise it would only have been another help in the piggery or the stables, which' ... a sigh ... 'certainly is needed.'

'I'll help,' Catty had offered eagerly, for she had loved Mother and Roger equally on sight. But when she had visited the stables she had had a second mind on that, and Roger had put his hands on his hips and laughed.

'They don't eat small girls,' he had assured her.

But to a small girl whose only association with a horse had been on fête days when she had been treated to rides on the merry-go-round, it was not sufficiently cheering. She had backed out and Mother had shaken her head at Roger, and he had nodded back to her, because ... and a rush of love now encompassed Catty ... they had been understanding people like that.

Perhaps she might have overcome her dislike had the thing not happened ... or had not happened to Roger, Roger her idol. She had heard Roger's voice calling from the barn, and something in it had pushed aside her nervousness and sent her racing across the lawn.

Roger was in the box with the new stallion and he looked white and strained. Something had disturbed the stallion and it was striking nervously with its hoofs.

'Get Horsley,' he had called, but before she had turned,

Roger had been struck. Her screams had brought the groom without her having to leave Roger. The man had got the stallion out and Catty had run to lift Roger's head on to her lap. Mother had come . . . an ambulance. It had been touchy for a while, and Roger had been four months in hospital. He had come back to horses . . . it was through them that he had met Lilla, who was an accomplished equestrienne.

But Catty had never forgotten that day . . . and never liked horses.

'Yes, horses.' There was a bland smile quirking David Jasper's long mouth as though he knew her dread. 'You're experienced . . . *of course.*'

'No,' she said. She added, '*Of course.*'

'An English girl! Graduate of one of a thousand pony clubs!'

'Also,' she reminded him, 'a ward.'

'Ah, I forgot. Shame on me not to remember your early inadequacies, your heart-touching unprivileged state.'

'Evidently you were more fortunate in your institution, or were you only amusing yourself the other day when you said you, too, were one of the unbelonging?'

'Oh, no, it was true enough.'

'An orphanage running to ponies for the small boys,' she marvelled, determined to match his sarcasm.

'No,' he said a little shortly, 'the horses came later at my foster-home. But those institution ponies could happen. In fact they're happening here. The pony school at Emu Heights is putting in new hacks. They've donated the six they no longer require to Universe. So as well as other country benefits, the children will have horses. Tony will attend to the boys, you to the girls.'

'Oh, no!' The words were on her lips, but by some means that she would never know they did not escape any further.

'Even though you were not afforded the delight as a young child, as a young woman I presume you can ride.'

'Oh, yes.' This time the words did escape, and she

listened to them horrified. How could she lie so blandly, but of course, the reason was this man.

'Good, then. You can take alternate mornings with Tony. No need to produce any Olympic wonders, just so long as the girls can enjoy a canter—' Enjoy a canter! Catty felt quite sick.

He went soon afterwards, hoping, his expression inscrutable, that her lessons would not curtail her visits to the grove.

'I've had one visit.'

'Two,' he corrected.

'The first was an encounter.'

'But not a brief one.'

'You must be very interested to check up on me like this,' she said, and had the satisfaction of watching the dull red of annoyance ride up into his face.

'I'm interested in Universe, in the service rendered to it.'

'You need have no fear I shan't render every service.'

'Including continued boxes of oranges,' he baited. Before she could flash an angry rejoinder, he left.

But after he had gone the anger turned to dismay. How in heaven was she to overcome this? She could go to him and say: 'I can't ride and I'm afraid of learning.' But she knew she could not bring herself to do it, especially after she had just said blithely to his 'I presume you can ride?' a confident, 'Oh, yes.'

She clung to one hope. The girls. The girls could shrink from the prospect of riding, with a little subtle encouragement even refuse pointblank. That would end the matter. Even a severe person, and though he was firm Catty had to admit that Doctor David was also kind, would not persist.

In all fairness to Catty she did not decry the scheme when she announced it that night, but in all fairness she did not enthuse upon it either. She simply stated it unimportantly, and hoped for the best.

And lost.

They were all head over heels with excitement, fairly bursting to begin. She should have kept in mind, she thought ruefully, the instinctive rapport between a girl and a horse, even more so than a boy and a mount. Except that she had had that stallion episode eventually she might have been the same herself.

'Oh, a pony!'

'I'm going to gallop and gallop!'

'I'm going to hurdle!'

'I'm going to—'

'Girls, not so fast!' A pause. 'Is there any girl who feels she would like to stand down?' No answer. 'Don't be afraid to say. We'll understand.'

No answer.

'You, Marion?' Marion was a rather nervous child, she had taken the longest at swimming.

'Oh, Sister Pussycat, I can't wait!'

'Anne? Susan? Ann Mary?'

'Yes.' . . . 'Oh, yes.' . . . 'Yes, please!'

'Well, it seems you're all keen,' said Catty, never feeling less keen in her life. 'I'll look over your jeans, they'll have to do until we can manage jodhpurs.'

'When do we start?'

'The end of next week. The boys are learning now.' Catty had stipulated that on her own account, she simply had to have some time in preparation.

The next day, after the children had left for school, she spent a frenzied hour in the Universe library, frenzied because it seemed to touch on all sport except riding.

'Looking for something you can't find?' asked Mr. Chester, seeing her take out volume after volume. 'Why don't you try the bookmobile, it calls on Emu Heights today. It's Shire-run and very good. Mrs. Chester always goes down. If you tell her, she could get it for you.'

'Thank you,' said Catty, 'but you know how it is with books, you sort of have to browse.'

'Well, go down with her. There's nothing doing until the children get back.'

'Thank you,' appreciated Catty, 'I will.'

Mrs. Chester gave her passenger a rather hair-raising trip through the hills. She loved to talk, and it seemed that the part of the talk that needed emphasis with her hands always occurred at curves. But, she assured Catty, the car knew its way, anyway, and they arrived safely. A few moments later the bookmobile pulled in.

It proved a moderate-sized van with a small flight of easy stairs that folded out from its rear. Once you climbed the stairs a perfectly arranged miniature library awaited you, with laden shelves ranging from above eye level for the adults down to the floor for the tinies. A quick glance assured Catty that the contents were widely and wisely selected.

She had no fear that Mrs. Chester would look at her choice, like all book people only their own choice mattered, they stepped out of themselves and became someone else, they weren't even here. Mrs. Chester wasn't here. She liked historical romances, and when Catty asked was she ready to leave, looked up with surprised eyes, so that Catty knew she was mingling with the ladies of one of the Tudor courts, or one of the Stuarts, or—

'I have to get a book on cricket for Mr. Chester,' said Mrs. Chester, and took up the first on the shelf.

Catty held her own book *How to Ride a Horse* with its cover held inward.

When they got back to Camp Universe, Catty walked over to the enclosure where the horses were corralled. Even to her inexperienced eye they looked quiet, and coming as they did from a riding school they would have to be, otherwise they would not be tolerated. So thank goodness at least for that.

Tony came up behind her and said feelingly, 'It was good of the pony club, I suppose, but I would have preferred something you didn't have to start with a smack on the rump.'

Catty listened keenly, determining never to smack any of them on the rump, or at least to make it a very little

93

smack, simply enough to get going.

'Which is the mildest?' she asked, adding quickly that she was thinking of Ann Mary.

'I'd say that bay with the sack over his barrel, though speaking of barrels, they're all grossly over-grassed.'

'I see,' Catty said, making note of the bay.

When she got to Sky House, she took herself to her room, closed the door and began to study. She did not care at all for the primary note of advice, that of riding first without a saddle so as to ensure the close relation feeling. She wanted no close relation.

She learned all about mounting. Gripping, yet not consciously so, with the knees. About not taking hold of the mane. Grasping the reins firmly yet not tightly. It all sounded easy on paper, but how would it be on the back of a horse? She shuddered.

She listened to the children's pony chatter that night and felt worse than ever. If only they were not so unanimous about it, if only there was one of them to creep up to her and confide, 'I'm scared, Sister Pussycat.' If there had been, she knew she would have been braver. At least she could not have felt totally inadequate as she did now.

Somehow she got through the night, got through the hours to school departure the next morning, then, the moment the bus turned the corner, she got into her slacks and went tremblingly to the paddock. Previously she had seen Tony leaving for Emu Heights, and she knew that Mr. Chester would be cloistered in his office.

She wished she had asked the name of the bay, she supposed horses were like dogs and answered to their name. She tried a few likely ones, but nothing happened, so in the end she went across and got hold of the bay. He looked completely surprised as though such a thing had never happened to him in all his life, yet it must have happened many times in a riding school.

Gritting her teeth in determination, trying not to be sick with fear, she did as the textbook advised, mounted the horse without a saddle. Now, according to *How to Ride a Horse,* came the close relations. Well, all she could say was the horse apparently did not feel it, while she, the rider, first of all hung to the mane, then remembered she shouldn't, hung with her knees, then remembered she shouldn't, then simply hung. How, she would never know.

But slowly, fearfully, something came, and she knew she would still be on if the horse moved a little faster than it was moving now. She tried it, and after five minutes she was still there, still on. That was enough for today. She got giddily off and went back to Sky House.

She studied the second chapter on saddling. She knew where the saddles were kept and the next day she tried Russet, as she called him, without the close relation of knees against warm horseflesh. She went a little faster.

On the third day she knew she was improving. Her heart didn't race so sickeningly. She wasn't so gaspy. The perspiration did not trickle so icily down her back.

The fourth day, though still a nightmare, found her riding in a rough sort of rhythm instead of jolting up and down, and she was so encouraged she went back in the afternoon and rode for an hour.

That night she could hardly drag herself across to dinner. After she had bedded the girls she soaked for a long time in a hot salt tub, but the next day she was even worse.

She knew she moved stiffly, but hoped it did not notice. Children's eyes missed little, though. Ann Mary said, 'You look like my robot man, Sister Pussycat, except you're a girl.'

'You do seem stiff, Sister Pussycat,' agreed Anne, their little nurse. 'Are you all right?'

'You have rumsticks,' diagnosed Ann Mary. 'My grandmother had rumsticks. The grandmother with your face.'

'Rheumatics. I'm quite all right, girls.'

But she still could not stop herself grimacing every time

she sat down.

'It's your bot,' pounced Ann Mary. 'My grand-mother—'

'Ann Mary, stop chattering! I'm quite all right.'

It was Doctor Jasper's night for the next chapter on Bettina, the spacewoman.

Catty went into her room and sank painfully down on the bed. Outside she could hear David's voice, the occasional enthralled gasp of the girls as they heard more about the intrepid Bettina.

She must have dozed – riding certainly exhausted you – for the first she knew that Doctor Jasper was standing beside her was when he took her wrist in his.

'Pulse satisfactory,' he proclaimed drily. 'Put out your tongue.'

'I'll do nothing of the sort. What nonsense is this?'

'The girls have been telling me you're not well.'

'I'm perfectly well.'

'You're not hot,' he agreed, 'your pulse-rate is normal, but what about the pain?'

'I have no pain.' – Well, she hadn't. Just a stiffness that made her feel, like Ann Mary's robot, that she would need to be wound up to move again.

'I'm told there is one,' he said. He paused. 'I was told where.' He paused again. 'By Ann Mary.'

She felt the blood coursing into her cheeks. Rumsticks, the youngest had said. It's your bot.

'How modest we are,' he was saying, and she knew that Ann Mary indeed had detailed her diagnosis. 'Will you show me where?'

'No.'

'I'm not asking you to mark it with an X, just point and I can tell you whether it's lumbago or—'

'It's nothing. Nothing!' Catty knew her voice had risen, but she could not care. She got up from the bed and moved blithely . . . she hoped . . . to the door. 'Goodnight, Doctor Jasper. At this time of evening I always give myself a breath of evening air.' She added as he took a step after her, 'Alone.'

She managed to get out quite fluidly, managed to make the shadow of a tree. But there she leant against the trunk and cursed all horses who caused pains like this, all doctors who came to investigate the pain, all little girls who diagnose, and make public, the offending spot.

When all was clear at last she went stiffly back to Sky House and another saline soak, for tomorrow she had to go through it all again.

And she went through it, through every agonizing jerk and pain-arousing jolt, but she could feel herself loosening up and she knew she would never be stiff like that again.

Encouraged, in the afternoon she returned to the enclosure, and feeling quite confident now, saddled Russet and actually rode him out of the corral.

Around the paddock, she had planned, even as far as the first gully . . . but Catty was to learn otherwise.

Scarcely had she closed the gate behind her than Russet got into a different rhythm altogether. Instead of the pleasant up and down, her reins holding him, her knees holding her, the horse took over. Useless for Catty to pull back, to try to turn or veer him, Russet had a goal in view, and nothing and nobody was going to stop him.

Down the valley he cantered, across the flat, Catty calling, 'Stop, Russet . . . bad Russet . . . whoa, you big bully!' Russet just went on.

It came to Catty as they dipped down another gully that Russet was going home to the pony school. That eagerness could not be put down to anything else. She sympathized with the horse, for home was home, but she sympathized more for herself. The pony school was dead in the middle of Emu Heights, Emu Heights being that sort of rustic place, and it was the time of day when Doctor Jasper would be at his surgery. He would be sure to see her, and what sort of idiot would she look being borne along by a homing horse, incapable of halting or turning him back, she who had answered his 'I presume you can ride?' with an airy, 'Oh, yes.'

'Russet, *darling*,' she appealed.

It was no use. Russet was smelling the smells of old, he was giving out excited snorts and increasing his pace. He actually leapt over a creek bed and to her surprise Catty was on him when he got to the other side.

They came out of the bush almost into the town's single street, and Russet, seeing the end in sight, began to gallop.

Vaguely, for it was taking all her time and all her knee-hugging to remain on, Catty was aware of the towns-people looking at her, then of someone coming to a surgery door and—

There was a gate rising up, the gate to the pony school. It was closed.

'If you stop I'll open it, Russet,' Catty called urgently. 'I'll *open* it, do you hear, you – you horse!'

But Russet hadn't time for things like that, bracing himself he took an infinitesimal halt, one of those halts, Catty knew sickeningly, that portended something, and she had a fair idea what it was going to be.

It was.

Over the gate they went, and like at the creek bed, on the other side she was still on. Russet was whinnying, and moving to where he remembered his feed bag had hung. The pony school owner and two grooms were running out and staring as though they had never seen such a thing before.

'Where in tarnation did you find him?' gasped the three of them. 'Given him up, we had.'

'How on earth did you ride him? That feller is murder,' added one of the grooms fearfully.

'He's from Camp Universe. You donated him to us,' puffed Catty.

'Oh, that's what happened.' This was Mr. McWhirter, the principal. 'I wondered why Billy Boy was still here and Red Fury gone.'

'R-red F-fury?' she echoed.

'Him,' nodded Mr. McWhirter. 'A wild boy if I ever saw one.'

'But isn't he a hack?'

'A hack? The Fury? a *hack*! – Are you all right, miss?'

Miss was not all right. She was sliding down the bay's back. She was lying prone on the ground.

When she awoke she was in the surgery on a couch, and David Jasper was saying, 'So that was why you had a pain in a particular spot.'

'I was teaching myself to ride.'

'On a tough horse?'

'I didn't know, I . . .' Catty kept still and wished desperately what seemed imminent to happen wouldn't happen, but it was no use.

'I think,' she said, 'I'm going to be sick.'

She was.

He was very professional. As a nurse she noted he did not skip one step. He supported her while nausea followed nausea, he made the accepted soothing sounds with his throat. When she was finished he let her stay exhausted where she was, not removing her to somewhere cool and clean until some of her depletion and weakness had gone.

Then he put her on a bed, and she realized with some surprise that he lived behind the surgery. He went away to come back with a towel and some warm water. He was infinitely gentle as he cleaned up her face and hands. He wrung out a cloth in cold water this time, laid it over her brow, told her to close her eyes and left her a while.

When he returned he had a clean shirt for her, much too big, he said, but if she tucked it into her pants . . .

'No, thank you.'

'That one is disgusting. It will make you sick again.'

'No, I won't be sick.'

'Then I shall.' To her horror he started unbuttoning her blouse.

'It's all right . . . I mean I'm all right . . . I mean . . .'

'You mean you don't want me to put you into it? Please yourself, Sister Quentin, but' . . . with emphasis . . . 'it has to go on.'

She struggled up to a sitting position, then when he went to support her, shrank away. He smiled lopsidedly but still stood there.

'Turn around, please,' she said.

He turned. She had a horrible suspicion he was suppressing laughter, for his shoulders went up and down.

'All right,' she said presently in a small voice.

'I'll bring in some coffee.' He did not go to his surgery coffee machine from which he handed out paper cups to patients who needed relaxation, needed something to hold in nervous hands, he went to his kitchenette, and the brew he brought back was much stronger than before. It was also very sweet. She knew that was for shock, so did not complain.

He waited until she had taken a few sips, then he said warmly, 'Whatever else I have to say to you, I have to say first that that was a grand effort for someone who is inexperienced, who, as you've told me, can ride, but no more.'

Somehow she knew she must tell him the truth. Though she felt much more confident now than she had a week ago, she must still in all fairness admit her incapability to him, let him judge her future teaching rôle.

'But I couldn't,' she said.

His brows were meeting. 'Couldn't what?'

'Couldn't ride.'

'You mean you couldn't ride when you told me you could?'

'Yes.'

'So you set out to teach yourself?'

'Yes.'

'On a horse like Fury?'

'I told you I didn't know.'

'And *I* am telling you something, Sister Quentin: If I

had my way that spot that Ann Mary told me of would be a whole heap sorer. You utter little fool, don't you see what could have happened?'

'It didn't happen,' she pointed out.

'To what miracle do you put that?'

'No miracle. I read the book. It was *How to Ride a Horse*, and I borrowed it from the bookmobile. Chapter One said no saddle at first to ensure a close relation feeling.'

'Did you get the feeling?'

She shook her head ruefully. 'Another feeling.'

'Not nearly hard nor stinging enough,' he glowered. 'Go on.'

'There's no more. I just practised every day. Then today I felt confident enough to leave the corral and go round the paddock. Only Russet—'

'Russet?' he asked.

'Fury . . . had other ideas.'

'Were you scared?' Had she looked up she would have seen that his eyes were gentle now.

'No, not so much scared as embarrassed. I could see that Russet . . . Fury was making for home, and I could imagine you at the surgery door laughing at me.'

'I wasn't laughing,' he said gravely.

'I'm sorry to have caused all this trouble,' she submitted humbly.

'By the looks of the townspeople they were extremely entertained, and the pony proprietor and his grooms are very pleased to have Fury back. He is, I believe, quite an expensive hunk of horse.'

'Then why is he at the school?'

'He's a boarder, not a member. He was supposed to be relaxing before an intensive professional training. Great things are expected of him, he comes from an illustrious lineage.'

'He's going to be a – racehorse?' she said, petrified.

'Yes. Are you going to be sick again?'

'No.'

'Well, *I* am sick, Sister Quentin. Sick at the thought that you couldn't come to me and say: "I can't . . . I don't know how . . . Please cancel me out." Am I that much of an ogre?'

She shook her head.

'Then why? *Why?*'

But all she answered was: 'I don't know.'

He left it at that at last and said he would take her back.

'I can go myself,' Catty said.

'On the substitute horse, Billy Boy, wasn't it? The hack which should have been there all along.'

She thought about that, but knew she couldn't face another ride, not so soon.

'I'll walk.'

'As far as the car,' he agreed, 'though I'd sooner carry you.'

'The townspeople—'

'Would be entertained again. Emu Heights is very rural, they don't get much diversion like this.'

'I'll still walk to the car.' She got up, felt wobbly but managed to conceal it, and went carefully out.

About to step into the car, something impelled her to look across to the riding school. A well-remembered head leaned over the top bar of the fence; she should remember it, she had clung mercilessly to its mane for the first agonizing days. 'Oh, Russet,' she said, a foolish lump in her throat.

Then a remarkable thing happened – remarkable, anyway, according to the pony people who told David and Catty afterwards that never, *never* had the Fury been anything but unfriendly and morose. The bay whinnied, whinnied at Catty, and all at once she was forgetting her weakness and running across to take his nose in her hand and climb up to kiss his brow.

'Miss, he's dangerous,' called a groom.

'Miss, keep back!'

But Catty knew differently, the bay knew differently.

If David Jasper knew anything, he did not tell. He just waited and watched ... watched a fair head against a nuzzling chestnut-red one. Two soft blue and two deep brown eyes.

CHAPTER SIX

THE girls embraced riding far more easily than they had embraced swimming. Though they had learned that art they had never really taken to it like 'fish to water', and though 'born to the saddle' would have been an equal exaggeration, what they lacked in riding know-how they made up for in eager enthusiasm, something that Catty had had to whip up anew every swimming day. She supposed it was the weather; spring was so uncertain, particularly at Emu Heights where a wind could come whistling razor-edged down from the Great Divide. At such times the blue pool took on a metallic look, and Catty did not blame her children for preferring the warm back of a co-operative pony.

She had been delighted to discover how co-operative. These horses had known no other life than that of jogging people along country tracks. Little people with their welcome low weights suited them admirably, and they carried their burdens for all the world as though they were merry-go-round steeds moving to a merry air.

Standing with Tony watching them, Catty had complained feelingly: 'And you recommended Red Fury!'

Tony laughed. 'I was going by the bag over him, I thought he must be getting on in years. But why are you complaining? He certainly taught you to ride.'

'But ride only Russet,' she sighed wistfully. 'I just can't take to these fellows after Rus.'

It soon evolved that Russet felt the same. One morning Mr. Chester sent for Catty, and when she got to the office there awaited the pony school proprietor. He had a request to make.

Red Fury, he admitted, was really worrying them. They had accepted him from a rich client for a period of rest, build up and moderate exercise. The first two they had availed the Fury, but moderate exercise they had not availed for the simple reason that Fury would not allow either of the grooms, both experienced men, on his back.

'We don't want to lose this client, miss,' the pony man said.

'I had no trouble with Russet . . . I mean with Fury.'

'That's what I've come about.'

The pony man then asked if Catty would consider riding Fury sometimes, for a fee, of course.

Catty would gladly have paid to ride him, and even began to say so, but Mr. Chester came in resourcefully that as Miss Quentin would be exercising the horse in Universe time she could not, of course, receive payment, but on the other hand a donation to the Camp . . .

'Done,' said the pony club man.

Everyone was pleased, Catty slyly pleased to be in the same contributing category as Mrs. Frances, which should do much to help her lose that uneasiness in the woman's presence that she had known ever since the bikini affair . . . pleased most of all to renew Russet's friendship. She went down the next day, experienced the thrill of having the bay gallop across instantly to her call, and after that it was the close relationship that the book had promised, the love of a rider for a horse and a horse for its rider.

She followed all the foothill trails, very lovely trails, cool gullies where trees grew tall and where grey moss tasselled down their trunks in silver wisps, man-made breaks in the tree tapestry intended for future pea fields and pumpkin acres, where the woodsmoke from the fires the men doing the clearing for roads to lead there had lit, now spiralled up blue and tangy.

It was in one of these clearings she met David Jasper one morning, his stout little car bogged in the sticky red clay churned up by a bulldozer that had passed through after rain.

'Thank heaven!' he greeted her. 'I was wondering how

I could get out.'

She looked around, puzzled. The track was little more than merely designed as yet, it led nowhere, so why was he here at all?

'I had a little time,' he admitted, 'so I thought I would see what the shire was doing down here. It's a favourite spot.'

'You should have walked.'

'I know that now. Had you not come along—'

'You'll still have to walk.'

'I have a call to make at Burley's grove.' He looked anxiously at his watch.

'I'd like to help you,' Catty said coolly ... why not? he was always cool to her ... 'but I doubt if Russet would allow you to ride him even if—

'Oh, yes, I've heard about that one horse–one rider arrangement,' he said impatiently.

'Even if,' she finished, ignoring him, 'you rode behind me.'

'To which you also would object. It entails a certain seating arrangement, Sister Quentin. In short, it's very *near.*'

'As well as too heavy for Russet. I'm sorry, Doctor Jasper. Could I tell the Burleys you'll be along as soon as you can?'

'No, but you can take the end of this rope and have the horse pull me out.'

'Russet pull a car out?'

'It's not a heavy car and I have it half out already. I'll be at the back pushing, so you needn't be concerned.'

'I *am* concerned.'

'Yes, about the horse. I've been hearing all about that. So there *is* some love still there, Sister Quentin.'

She said stiffly, 'If you're sure there'll be no strain—'

'Take the rope,' he answered, 'and when I call out, move forward.'

She obeyed, but not enthusiastically. However, it was not such a tug, as he had promised, and the car grunted a moment, then cleared itself.

'Thanks,' he said.

'Thank Russet.'

He complied, poker-faced. 'Thank you, Russet.'

He still did not move away, and she waited a little uneasily, aware that although Mr. Chester was well pleased over her exercising of the bay, Mr. Chester was not a Board member. She braced herself for his censure, a censure she intended to throw back at this hard man with a proud announcement of the amount of the pony school's donation.

However, when he spoke it was not in that strain at all.

'You like this country?'

She looked around the shallow valley, spring green except where the clay-red road had been cut in, sloping upward to the top of the hill in chequered alternate patches of pink pudding weed and gold four o'clocks to finish at an almost periwinkle blue sky, and breathed, 'Oh, yes!'

'I love it, too.'

'Yet you'll leave it?'

He looked at her in inquiry, and she quoted Bevan Bruce's: 'You can't keep men like David Jasper in a background like this.'

'To whom do I bow?' he asked coldly.

'Couldn't I have said it myself?'

'No.'

'You're right. Mr. Bruce said it.'

His hand was on the ignition. 'See a lot of him?'

'Is it forbidden?'

'I asked you a question.'

Annoyed, she pulled on Russet's rein to go away, but a quick firm hand emerged through the car window space to pull the rein the other way.

'I wouldn't do that,' she said sharply. 'You must have heard how the grooms fared with Red Fury.'

'Oh, I've heard about this fellow as a one-girl horse,

but relationships like that can be grown out of. For instance, I know some one-man girls who eventually have second thoughts.' He was looking at her narrowly.

'I don't think Russet has those ideas,' she said.

'And you?'

'What are you talking about, Doctor Jasper?'

'Memories,' he reminded her, and she knew he was referring to that day when she had answered him stiffly that she had no lover, but had admitted on his ruthless probing to memories. Memories, had he known it, of her little lost ones. Roger's babies. She bit down on her lip, and he laughed softly.

'You and Fury, too. – The brute is trying to bite me. Away with you, one-girl horse, and with you, Sister Quentin, with your one-man dream. I have the Burley call to make.' He started the engine and manipulated the car carefully back along the uncompleted road. He did not look at her.

On her return journey to leave Russet at the stables . . . either the proprietor or one of the grooms always drove her up to Universe . . . Catty rimmed the Sunny Wonder grove. She was on a different side of the property to the side she usually took, this side was entirely filled in with established trees that should need little attention apart from the light weeding to keep the ground 'open' and the moderate fertilizing, which was all, she had learned, that citrus would tolerate, so it was a surprise to see Bevan at work on these rows.

She pulled on Russet's reins and called out to the orchardist: 'Are you cropping?' She knew now because of the different strains there could be fruit every month.

He got up from where he was kneeling beside a trunk, smiled and came to her.

'No,' he said, 'actually I was considering, Catriona.'

'Something serious?'

'It could be. I have a feeling, don't ask me why, just put it down to an orange man's hunch, that we're going to have a freeze.'

'A freeze? Oh, Bevan, don't be absurd.'

'Unfortunately I'm being wise. It's still spring, remember, and spring's capricious. I've been watching that cloud.'

She looked where he was pointing and saw nothing to alarm her, but then, she told him, she was not an orange man.

'If you were an orange man's wife, you'd see,' he said hopefully, but she steered him away from that.

'Tell me what you're afraid of.'

'Well, not a freeze perhaps, I mean in this latitude there couldn't, or shouldn't, be, but a sudden severe drop in temperature, followed, as is likely in this season, by an abundance of hot sun.'

'Wouldn't that help?'

'It could kill the trees, Catriona.'

'Can't anything be done?'

'Yes, stop the freeze, or whatever it is.' He laughed ruefully. 'Next best to that, get out the whitewash.'

'Whitewash?' she queried.

'Done at once after an injury it lessens the effect. Every hour of exposure matters. I should have seen to it in the winter, but how could I know . . .' He glanced up at the warning he could see and Catty could not.

'Have the Universe boys protected their little grove?' she asked.

'Oh, yes, Catriona, I'm a good instructor.'

'Then they can come down and start on teacher's.'

'They wouldn't think much of my methods,' he sighed, 'telling them what to do but not doing it myself. No, I couldn't call on them.'

'Then you can call on Sky House,' she said. 'The girls will love it. How many brushes do you have?'

'Catriona!' For Catty was urging Russet away.

'Fifteen . . . twenty . . . how many?' she called.

'What a girl!' was all he answered back.

As she had told him, her girls could not wait to go down to the grove to splash around the whitewash. Mr.

Chester, when Catty had asked him, had been all approval, even unearthed some old brushes to supplement Bevan's supply.

'He's kept us in citrus,' he appreciated, 'and he's spent so much time instructing the boys it's no wonder he slipped up on his own trees.'

'Is it usually done?'

'In the manual,' confirmed Mr. Chester, 'and Bruce would teach the boys by that method, but no, it's not usual, our climate is too mild not to permit a risk.'

'It looks the same mildness to me now.'

'An orchardist can tell,' said the manager. 'I only hope he can be wrong, too.'

'Then I have your blessing?'

'Also these brushes and old gloves.'

'Gloves?'

'Bevan Bruce will tell you as you work,' Mr. Chester advised. 'If you go now you should get in some hours before it's dark.'

'And I do have your blessing?' she persisted.

'What is this?' he laughed.

'Not what,' corrected Catty gloomily. 'Doctor Jasper.'

'Who would be complete approval, vitamin C and all that. Now get going.'

Down at Sunny Wonder, which was only a ten-minute run along the bush track, Bevan had his own brushes waiting and a pile of gloves.

As the girls began jubilantly splashing the trunks with whitewash, not so far removed, Catty smiled to herself, from their mud pie days, even though the ingredients now were white, she asked the young orchardist about the gloves.

'For their hands, Bevan?'

'They do protect them, but mainly I'm protecting my trees. I always insist that any croppers I happen to employ wear gloves because even a fingernail can stratch a fruit and a decay germ enter and start a mischief.'

It was amazing how many trees the squad got through, by the first darkling of the sky Bevan said they had broken its back.

'Whose back?' asked Ann Mary typically.

'That old cloud who is cooking up a heap of mischief,' Bevan answered, taking the youngest up in his arms and pointing to a sky that still, to Catty, seemed innocuous.

'Poor cloud,' said Ann Mary, 'I didn't want to break its back.'

Mr. Chester came down with the Universe bus to take the girls home. Catty seated them all, then, remembering she had not collected the Camp brushes and gloves, ran back to the barn. She had hardly entered the barn than she heard the bus take off. She ran out, calling, but it was too late; evidently the girls and Mr. Chester had not noticed she was not there, and did not hear her now. Well, it needn't matter, Bevan could run her up.

But when she went to find him in the house, he was not there, even the housekeeper was out. She came on to the verandah, puzzled, then paused in surprise. Something was happening that vindicated all the afternoon's feverish effort. One might quote latitudes, parallels, temperature ranges, weather pattern, point out that here at Emu Heights snow had never happened, but right now snow was. She stood enchanted watching it purl down. She caught her breath at the soft light, at the soft little sounds, at the soft covering on the ground. She saw the barn already roofed in white, marooned in white, the groves a sheet of white, the trees—

The trees! She put a halt to her enchantment. Bevan's citrus, how would it take to this?

Then she saw through the avenues that even this soon were tinkling frozen snow from laden branches to the ground that the citrus would not take it. Blue smoke was spiralling upwards from a dozen small fires, and Bevan and Mrs. Mallard were running from fire to fire to keep the flames alive. Of course, she accepted, if the temperature drops too much not only will the crop be ruined but the trees will be destroyed as well. She ran out and began grabbing the tinder that Bevan distributed, then sheltering and coaxing the unwilling fires he had lit, fanning the hard-won heat, almost *squeezing* out that heat, then directing it towards the trees.

Bevan threw her a grateful look and said between his efforts, 'Thank you for ever, Catriona.'

They worked like slaves for over an hour. Out of the distant bush more spirals of smoke appeared, and Catty knew that all the groves were toiling frantically to save their trees as well. Had this been a snow area, he would have been prepared, have had electrical equipment ready to switch on, probably never would have gone in for citrus at all, but the fall had taken them by surprise, the bad weather they had seen in the sky had not, in their wildest imagination, included *snow*. Even up in the coldest town of the Blue Mountains, snow was not an expected occurrence.

Then, as unexpected and as suddenly as it had appeared, the snow stopped. The temperature climbed. The snow slid off the trees. The puddles that had covered over with ice cracked open. Great falls of snow slid from the barn roof and almost at once became a small river. The icicles dripping from the verandah were water drops instead.

'It's over,' called Bevan, 'and now we begin.'

'Begin?'

'There'll be tree injuries. Not from the snow, but from the weight of it, branches will have broken off. You saw me bandaging the other day.'

She nodded.

'That's what we'll have to do now, otherwise the sun on top of this freak freeze tomorrow will destroy any wounded tree.'

He seemed to take it for granted she was here to help him, and why not? she thought; why shouldn't she remain and help him? He was a generous donor to Universe. Also, though this reason was not for the Board should they ask for a reason, she liked Bevan very much.

She walked beside him and was sorrowed when he pointed out three beautiful shaddocks that had received the worst of the impact, and would need to be destroyed. However, as they proceeded further, she saw that the rest of the grove had weathered quite well, that comparatively small repairs would need to be given.

He allotted her a damaged row, showing her how to repair spirally from the bottom of the tree to the top. She knew now the drill of the oiled gauze.

She worked steadily by torchlight, lamplight, firelight and actually now a bright moon, her fingers cold and clumsy at first but gaining agility as the temperature rose and the snow slid away. The time flew.

Somewhere she supposed Mrs. Mallard worked on the wounded trees as well, it would be all hands on deck, but it was not the housekeeper who met her at the end of a finished row just as her own row finished, it was Bevan. As naturally as sun after rain, as dawn after night, as nature itself, he took her in his arms and kissed her, and she found herself kissing him back. It was relief, she knew, it was a job well done, Mrs. Mallard who had just joined them must feel that, too.

It was several moments before Catty, who had only half seen, half sensed the third person who had joined them, realized it was not the housekeeper at all. It was a man. It was David Jasper. He stood smiling that narrow smile of his as he waited for them to withdraw from each other.

'All's well that ends well,' David Jasper suggested idly as they went back to the house. Ostensibly he was talking of the trees, but Catty knew there was an undercurrent here, and she resented it. After all because she was in the employ of Camp Universe was no reason that a Board member should censor what she chose to do, unless, of course, it affected the children under her care. But this had affected nobody, unless one counted the relief of an ordeal over finding release in two people's pleasure in what they had achieved.

The men were exchanging notes now, David Jasper reported that what had happened to Sunny Wonder had happened all over the groves.

'Only a little damage,' he said, 'they all lit up like you did.'

'Fortunately the market gardeners would not have their crops up to a vulnerable stage,' said Bevan, 'and as for the pumpkin people—'

' "When the frost is on the punkin",' quoted Doctor Jasper with a smile. 'The best pumpkins of all are frosty ones, so snow should do no harm.'

They had reached the house, and Mrs. Mallard who had gone on ahead had coffee and toast waiting.

The men still discussed the weather, the surprise the snow had been even up in the Divide so late in the spring. At Bevan's inquiry as to how Camp Universe had fared, David laughed and answered that no movie night ever had provided such entertainment. Undoubtedly the children wanted the snow to continue. There were several emergencies already in the pool.

'The pool! Don't tell me you had some stalwarts choosing a snowstorm to swim in?' disbelieved Bevan.

'Being inexperienced they believed the pool would have iced up, so tried to skate, or at least to slide. No, Sister Quentin' . . . as Catty looked anxiously across . . . 'it was none of your little dears. They were too consumed with worry over Sister Pussycat, who one minute was with them, they said, but the next—' He shrugged.

'I came back for the brushes and gloves,' said Catty unhappily. 'They mustn't have noticed, because they went without me.'

'No need for an explanation,' David Jasper assured her smoothly. 'I'm sure Bevan is glad that you did just that.'

'And more than that,' came in Bevan, 'Catriona and the girls spent the hours after school whitewashing.'

'I can believe it,' nodded David, 'from the splashes on them. At first I thought it was the snow.' He laughed.

Another censure, thought Catty of that edged laugh, this time for not being present to check my charges. She said of the silent censure that he was undoubtedly making of the whitewashing: 'We had Mr. Chester's blessing.'

'How nice,' David Jasper said.

Mrs. Mallard asked solicitously if the pool victims had been put into sick bay.

'They appear no worse, but I did prescribe just that, which pained them very much, since Camp Universe, being on a small plateau, has succeeded in pocketing quite a heap of snow. The rest of the children are snow-balling madly while the fun lasts.'

'My children?' said Catty anxiously, wondering if they were sufficiently wrapped up.

'Not when I left. They were too worried about Sister Pussycat. I just told you, Sister Quentin. Remarkable, really, how soon you have entangled yourself in their hearts ... that is—' another of the edged smiles – 'for someone who doesn't think that entangling way herself. Why, they even put off Chapter Nine of Bettina!'

Bevan was looking at them in a puzzled manner, and Catty said mechanically, 'It's a book about a space-woman,' knowing it answered nothing. But how, she thought angrily, could she explain that David Jasper was using his usual barbed line of a love that did not reach out any more because it was entailed with only one person? What had he said? A one-girl horse ... a one-man dream. But he had been wrong, it had not been a man but two children, Gaby and Georgie, and Lilla had taken them from her.

She heard the men talking again, but she did not follow their words. In spite of the heat of the room, the scalding coffee, she felt cold, and she knew it was not that coldness of deprivation that she always felt when she realized afresh her absence now and her future absence from Roger's children, but an actual physical coldness. Oh, no, she thought, I simply can't have a chill.

But the feeling worsened. It was all she could do not to shiver noticeably. She had to grit her teeth to stop the chattering. Her head ached. Her limbs felt heavy. So long as he doesn't see, she thought desperately, I can dose myself at Sky House. She talked brightly ... got up and served second cups. It was a remarkable feat, for her legs were jelly.

Then they were leaving in the doctor's car, and Catty was talking animatedly out of the window to Bevan and Mrs. Mallard. If I can only keep it up, she urged herself, David Jasper won't be able to recite all I've done wrong today, for I simply couldn't bear that now. Also, he won't see how wretched I feel.

'All right,' drawled the doctor, 'you can drop the pretence and sit back. Because' ... a pause ... 'you're sick, aren't you?'

'I'm not, I—'

'Sick,' he repeated. Then: 'Be quiet,' he said.

Thankfully, for the moment, anyway, she sat back.

She closed her eyes as they ascended to Camp Universe, but the children's laughter when the car turned into the drive sent them opening again.

It was a Christmas postcard scene that Catty saw, something that had never happened here before and possibly never would happen again. The Camp, with its plateau setting and sloping sides, had pocketed so much snow that it could have been situated in an alpine village instead of the lower foothills to a moderate range in the milder latitudes.

Snowballs were whizzing everywhere, snowmen outdoing each other in size and shape. Catty could see her own charges among the revellers and mentally thanked Mrs. Chester ... she supposed it would be Mrs. Chester ... for having wrapped them warmly, and for not having deprived them of the fun, for snow fun was like no other fun, she thought; a child should never be deprived, and particularly a warmer country child.

But David Jasper was shrugging meaningly. 'Little ingrates,' he said of the girls, 'typical women.'

'How do you mean?'

'All unselfish concern one minute, all selfish self-absorption the next. The false little beasts were actually in tears over you, Sister Pussycat, and now—' He waved an arm.

'They're only little girls,' she defended.

'Who grow into women.'

'Yes, that's a pity,' she agreed coolly. 'If you could arrange things undoubtedly you'd grow them into men.'

'A world of men,' he mused, pulling the car up at Sky House and apparently considering the idea. 'How would you like that? Or would you sooner' ... a pause ... 'a one-man world?'

'Oh, not that again!' She went to get out, but he forestalled the movement by coming quickly to her side of the car and lifting her in his arms.

'I'm all right. I can manage.'

'You're in for a bout, you know that, don't you, and I'm carrying you in and putting you to bed.'

'You're doing nothing of the sort!'

'Well, seeing you get into it,' he said impatiently, 'after which I'll do the usual aspirin and lemon routine. Have you lemons here?'

'In the fridge. But aspirins and lemon juice—'

'Pending shots I hope you won't need tomorrow. Are you sure you can get yourself to bed?'

'Of course,' hurriedly.

A smile. That narrow smile he could put on. 'Otherwise,' he concluded, 'I'd fetch Mrs. Chester.'

Red-cheeked from annoyance as well as a temperature that she suspected was rather high, Catty undressed and got into her cot. She lay back exhausted, too tired even to wonder how the children would bed themselves. He assured her, however, as he brought in steaming lemon and aspirin.

'Don't worry about the tots. I'll hear their prayers.'

'And tell them to "go",' she added foolishly. There must be something as well as aspirin in the hot toddy.

As if a long way off she heard him laughing . . . later heard returning steps, excited voices hushed at once to whispers, the sound of bath taps, the sound of slippered feet, then silence, and lights out.

No light at the foot of her bed to outline him, but she knew even in her half consciousness that he was there.

'Goodnight, Sister Pussycat,' he said.

She was worse in the morning. Dry-mouthed, burning-eyed, she lay there uncaring. Uncaring that the girls had to get themselves up and dressed for school. Uncaring about anything.

But once, dizzily, she thought that this must be the final straw, for Camp Universe, no Board would tolerate a house-mother who had been invalided twice in such a short period. But she did not think about it for long. She just closed her eyes and felt ill.

She was vaguely aware of ministering hands, but she was beyond finding out whose hands, though they were not, she knew, the same firm strong hands that took her up later and deposited her some time afterwards in another bed.

A hospital bed. She knew that when she opened her eyes and really saw at last.

'Thank heaven!' said a voice. 'I was beginning to think you needed some antibiotic that hasn't been discovered yet.' David Jasper sat on the bed beside her. 'I seem to be making a habit of this,' he remarked.

'Yes. I'm sorry.'

He shrugged that away. 'You couldn't help it, I suppose, and after all, keeping up the orange supply is pretty important.'

'Have I—'

'You've had pneumonia following a chill helping Sunny Wonder grove.'

'I'm sorry,' she said again.

She looked around her. It certainly seemed like a hospital ward, though there was something different about it.

'It's sick bay,' he said. 'You're still at Universe. That should help your convalescence. If the Board intended firing you they wouldn't heal you to do it first. No, they would send you to a public hospital.'

'Why wasn't I sent?'

'I told you. We're not firing you.'

'But seriously—'

'Seriously, you were not fit to travel. Seriously again, we had an excellent resident nurse.'

'A nurse?' she echoed.

He nodded to the door, and Anne, rising fifteen, came in. She wore the cap and apron Catty had made her for waitress, but with an entirely different air.

'Nurse Anne,' David introduced.

Anne put fruit juice down beside the patient, then proceeded to take Catty's temperature in a most professional way.

'Doctor David taught me,' she assured Catty in case she withdrew her hand. 'Before he did I was counting my own thumb.' She was gravely silent for a while, then she reported her finding to the doctor, saying, 'I think it's normal, sir.'

'It is,' said David.

'Aren't you going to check?'

'No, Nurse, I'm taking your word.'

'Oh, Doctor David!' Anne glowed. She went off to attend the other patients.

'Yes,' said David in answer to Catty's query, 'we have the would-be skaters in as well.' He laughed. 'It's a punishment as well as a precaution. I don't think those boys will try to skate on ice before it's properly ice again.'

'Where is the punishment?' asked Catty, looking appreciatively around at her bright comfort.

'Anne,' David grinned. 'Having to call her Nurse.'

He told Catty she must remain in sick bay a little longer. 'There's been meningitis down on the plain.'

'But I feel fine,' she protested.

'You'll stop, though,' he frowned. 'Pneumonia is first cousin to that other. Besides, Anne could not bear to be relieved this soon.'

'The boys—' she began.

'They're due to go. I only detained them to drive home the lesson. Imagine stepping into a pool and expecting ice!'

'When can I—'

'You're in a hurry, aren't you? Everything is functioning the same in your absence.'

'That's what I'm afraid of.'

'I told you you're not being fired.' He got up. 'You're to stop until Wednesday, anyway, because the girls are planning to visit you in the proper manner, flowers and offerings and the rest, and by the time fourteen of them have done that . . .'

'My darlings!' she said spontaneously.

'Darlings? Is this our detached house-mother who permits no such thing as love?'

'You won't ever forget that, will you?'

'I don't come into it, you do. Will you forget?'

'Doctor David,' called Nurse Anne, 'I think that Trevor has a slight rise. Will you come?'

'Till Wednesday,' repeated David Jasper. He followed Anne to the adjoining ward.

It was pleasant relaxing in Camp Universe sick bay. Through the window Catty could look down on Emu Heights, and beyond them to the green ribbon of the river. The voices of the children came musically to her ears. Children's voices were always musical when you were not near them, and probably, Catty smiled to herself, that distance established the music now. Also, Anne was a very good nurse. Catty heard her managing the boys in the next ward, being, and without instruction, adaptable, patient, discreet yet firm, those first golden rules of nursing.

When Anne came in and sat with her later she praised the girl and Nurse Anne flushed with pleasure.

'Oh, Sister Pussycat, it's the only thing I want. But' . . . face clouding . . . 'she'll never let me.'

'Your mother?'

'Yes.'

'But while you're here, darling—'

'I won't be,' said Anne bleakly. 'I'll be leaving. I'm fifteen next month.'

'But you don't have to leave.' Catty had learned that from Mr. Chester, he had said that a child could stop to adulthood, even after that if work could be found near at hand.

'She'll want me when I can earn something,' said Anne hopelessly. 'It's always like that.'

'No, it isn't, Anne.'

'It will be with my mother.'

Catty diverted the girl with nursing talk, and Anne responded at once. She was, Catty sincerely believed, that rare person: a born nurse.

When the children arrived after school to visit her, they were ushered in quietly, kept strictly to four at a time, and allowed no longer than five minutes.

They brought little nosegays of their own making, which Anne arranged in a vase, and which, no doubt, she would correctly remove before lights out.

Deborah proffered, 'My mother went into hospital to get me.'

Marion said condescendingly, 'My mother grows her own babies.'

This was the signal for a conversation which decided Catty that as soon as she was back at Sky House she would have some private talks with her girls. She smiled secretly at Anne rising fifteen, but Nurse Anne was watching the clock prior to telling the present quartet to leave and ushering in the next.

Bevan visited her, concerned that she had caught the chill helping him, only relaxing when she insisted that she was enjoying all this.

Mrs. Chester came, pleased that the sick bay was in use. 'I don't mean I'm pleased you're ill, Sister, but it's a beautifully equipped little hospital and up to now we haven't had a patient.'

'Now you have two wards occupied,' smiled Catty.

'The boys have been dismissed, there really wasn't anything wrong with them.'

'And there isn't with me now. I must get back to work.'

'It all depends on Doctor Jasper,' Mrs. Chester reminded her. She added warmly as Anne came in with a tray of tea: 'And Nurse.'

Undoubtedly Nurse would have liked to have kept Catty captive much longer, but when David next visited the patient he directed her back to work.

Catty was pleased to go, but Anne took off her cap and apron sadly.

'But you must go back to school, Anne, to get your entrance exam,' Catty reminded her. 'Every student nurse must pass that.'

'It won't be any use,' said Anne, 'I'll never be. She won't let me.'

'You can start training even when you're a woman. I know it sounds a long way off, but—'

'I'll never be,' was all Anne said again ... and Catty was to remember those words.

CHAPTER SEVEN

IT was lovely to be with her children once more. Catty
was glad that Doctor Jasper was not there to witness her
return, otherwise he would have made that edged remark
about love still existing again, and, gathering the girls
around her, she knew she would have had no defence.

For he was right. She found herself listening afresh for
Ann Mary's very young but often wise observances,
watching for the fleeting changes in Deborah's vulnerable
face, sensing Marion's unsureness, Lesley's hopes, Susan's
need for encouragement, feeling all their love . . . giving,
though she had tried not to, her love in return.

This was living life as it should be lived, giving love to
children and accepting it back from them. She had resolved not to, but it had been no use. Dear Gaby and dear
Georgie, forgive me, she smiled to the photo wallet.

'Who are they?' asked Ann Mary jealously. 'I don't like
those kids.'

'You would, though, darling, and they would like
you.'

'When are they coming?'

'They're not.'

'Then they have mothers and fathers,' deduced Ann
Mary.

'Yes.' – But have they, asked Catty sadly of herself,
have they? Or are they just two children in a good
school?

She put the wallet away. 'What has been happening?'
she asked.

'We're up to Chapter Eleven,' called Adrienne.

'Bettina, the Spacewoman?'

'Yes. Oh, Sister Pussycat, it's so thrilling. She's landed,
you know.'

'On the moon?'

'Yes.'

'Successfully, I hope.'

'We don't know till Twelve.'

'And that will be tonight.'

So David Jasper was expected, Catty thought.

'What else happened?' she asked.

'Visiting day,' they chorused.

'Anything special there?'

'Mardi's aunt brought a big cake, we all had some, and Mardi is going home soon.' Mardi was their on-loan child, daughter of road accident victims. Catty was happy for Mardi that her parents had recovered sufficiently to plan their family reunion.

'Did Anne's mother come?' Typical of Anne, she was in the dormitory turning down the beds. If Mrs. Meekes had, Catty thought, she had not crossed to the infirmary to visit her daughter, which meant she did not approve of Anne acting nurse. Catty sighed.

'No, she missed out,' they chorused, and Ann Mary added, 'If she comed I was going to tell her that Anne was dead.'

'Ann Mary!'

'Well, she doesn't love her,' Ann Mary said.

'That's quite enough now. There's something I want to talk about.' Catty had decided during her convalescence that she would clear up that hospital-grown baby of Deborah's mother.

She found her girls endearingly easy to speak to, and looking down on the fresh flower faces turned trustingly up to her, she remembered Mother talking in such a way years ago, and her heart went out to these small ones as she knew now Mother's heart had gone out to her. I *am* involved, she realized.

She was not aware that David Jasper had arrived for Chapter Twelve until she heard a choke of laughter from the corner of the room, quickly directed the other way. Belinda, whose mind was more inquiring than the rest, more factual, more in need of the black and white instead of the grey that Catty supposed she had been painting, had ferreted from Sister Pussycat *all* the pertinent details, not just the generalities, and now she said feelingly: 'There's two in our family. Fancy my poor mother having to go through that twice!'

It wasn't quite the effect Catty had wanted, but she left it at that for the present; after all, Belinda was very young. Also, she was burningly aware by the choked laugh that David Jasper had been listening to her facts of life.

He did not comment, though, and, as she had done previously, she took a walk outside while the remarkable Bettina achieved another lunar feat.

The freak snow had finished the capricious weather and now the days were blue and golden as spring touching summer days should be.

The girls' swimming had so improved that they were allowed to bathe at any time, being considered sufficiently proficient to give back any rough treatment they were given. How Mrs. Frances considered this, Catty did not know, but the boys' gym had gone up and she did not think she would remove it. Also, Dorothea of the bikini did not frequent the pool, only the hospital, for she was beginning a hospital-romance stage, and saw herself in all sorts of heart-throbbing situations. Anne, of course, was always there, but her dreams were different.

'A born nurse,' said Mrs. Chester to Catty, and Catty agreed, wondering why she felt a sudden tightness in her heart. After all, even if Anne's mother did put her to something else, if the girl still felt the same later on, she could start then. She had told Anne so. – And Anne had said: 'I'll never be.'

Catty wished she could stop remembering the bleak little voice.

The weeks into summer went pleasantly and uneventfully. The boys' section now had become so used to the girls' company, at meals, in the pool, riding, that they would have been startled to have found themselves once more only among males, just as they had been surprised a month ago at a sudden influx of females. If Our Founder could have seen them all now, Catty often thought, he would have been pleased. Life was as it should be lived, this was what he had wanted.

Bettina the Spacewoman was still doing remarkable things, and Catty was still taking the advantage of the doctor's continuing story to walk in the sweet late spring air.

One night she went further than usual, though ... as she told Bevan when she met him coming out of the Universe grove ... she could not have said why.

'Orange blossom,' he smiled.

'It's always there,' she told him, and that was a fact, there was always a tree in bloom.

'Ah, but it needs the right breeze to waft it. Tonight there's such a breeze. Take an enchanted breath, Catriona.'

She did, and she was enchanted. 'Is there anything in all the world like orange blossom?'

She saw from his expression that he was ready to answer that, so she asked quickly, 'Why are you here, Bevan? Surely not pruning by moonlight?'

'I left a pair of shears under a lime. I was demonstrating to the orchard class this afternoon and put them down, then didn't remember until dark. I would have waited till tomorrow, but they're a favourite pair.' He had put his fingers under her elbow to help her over a rough patch ... and left them there.

'Trees no worse for their freeze?' she asked for conversation, for she felt a little uncomfortable at the pressure of those fingers. Also tonight's Bettina must be drawing to a close, and she did not want to be seen with Bevan by Doctor Jasper. She thought of those narrowed eyes, that thinned mouth.

'No worse ... thanks to a guardian angel.' The pressure was tightened. 'Catriona, I—'

'Then you've no worries,' she inserted hurriedly.

Always the land man, Bevan was successfully diverted.

126

'No, not really, but the plains aren't so happy.'

'Why?' Now that she had his attention channelled to something else, she found herself interested, too, the earth and its problems had always interested her, Roger had said she would make a good farmer's wife.

'The market gardeners, I should have said,' Bevan told her. 'These plains are really only flats, riverlands, Catriona, river silt left over from floods have provided them with the rich soil they enjoy.'

'Then that's good.'

'Yes, but not the prospect of another flood.'

'Is there?' She was astonished; the days since the freak snow had been ideal.

'Where do you think all that melted water went?' he asked. 'Not just ours but the upper mountains in the Divide where the falls were really heavy.'

'I don't know,' she admitted.

'It went to swell up creeks and those creeks are naturally enough making their way down now. They'll be manageable if they stop in their present state, but if rains come . . .'

'Do they usually come at this time?'

'It's a predictably unpredictable country,' he shrugged. 'You are no longer in an ordered place of spring, summer, autumn, winter, where nature behaves as she should.'

'I know that,' she laughed. 'I was told before I came that in fall nothing fell.'

'You'll see for yourself in April, Catriona.'

'If I'm here.' She said the words idly, not prepared for his sudden release of her as he placed his two hands instead on her shoulder and shook her gently.

'If you're not here there'll be no orange blossom.'

'Oh, Bevan, you are poetic!' she smiled.

'Which evidently appeals to the lady more than science fiction. Good evening, Bruce. Good evening, Sister Quentin. I've been looking for you, Sister. The children now are unattended. Well – goodnight.' Doctor Jasper merged

127

into the night as suddenly as he had come out of it. The next moment they heard his car speeding down the drive.

'Bit abrupt,' Bevan commented.

'I really shouldn't have come this far. I must get back, Bevan.'

'Goodnight, orange blossom,' he said, and she knew he still stood there after she had gone. He was sweet, he was kind. She could think of nothing that was not nice about Bevan, so why was she thinking instead of narrowed eyes and a thinned mouth in an estimating face? It's because he represents my job, she told herself, as she ran back to Sky House.

But the next day she found ... and unpleasantly ... that she had others to answer to as well as Doctor David Jasper.

Mr. Chester came across soon after she had waved the children to school to inform her that there was to be a crash Board meeting.

'What's that?' she asked.

'My name for it, really. Regular Board Meetings are held here, and they are always pleasant predictable affairs. But we have this new member, Snedley, who has sat on other boards ... commercial boards ... and who insists on bringing commercial viewpoints into charity.'

'I think I understand. He believes in swoop inspections.'

'Well, you could say that in a way. So far he hasn't arrived entirely without warning, but he's been responsible for several inspections like this morning's, leaving us barely an hour for preparation.'

'Will the Board be here that soon?'

'Yes, my dear, and most of them ... well, the rest of them really ... will be kind and sympathetic. But Mr. Snedley ...' Mr. Chester looked worried.

'Is he liked by the others?'

'No.'

'Then why is he kept on the Board?'

'Why do we keep on the right side of Mrs. Frances?' sighed Mr. Chester in reply. 'Well, this won't get us anywhere. Mrs. Chester is checking the kitchen. I'm giving Fitz a word about the garden. Perhaps you could look over Sky House ... put a finishing touch here and there.'

'I will, I assure you,' encouraged Catty, and hurried in to the dormitories.

Although their domestic staff was very efficient Catty took the precaution of flicking around a duster. She filled vases with flowers that the gardener allowed her, then raided the toy cupboards and placed the dolls and teddy bears on the beds so that they sat neatly over the flannelette nighties, since flannelette, which was worn because the plateau nights grew chilly, was bulky. She distributed Nora's pile of books balancing perilously on the top of her bedside table ... Nora was their reader ... to other bedside tables. She straightened some mats, adjusted a curtain, pulled a blind—

And heard the approach of steps.

There were eleven of them in all, for Mr. Chester conducted them, and they mostly looked tolerant and benign. Catty remembered from her own childhood how to sort them out at a glance, the head-patters, the producers of sweeties from pockets, the penny-for-a-kiss fatherly figures, the chuck-under-chinners, the toss-in-the-air ones. But of course she was seeing from a child's eyes, a ward's eyes, her own eyes at ten years old; now she was a house-mother and she must sort them out differently. It was not hard, her first impression of tolerance and kindness repeated itself ... except for one member. The rest were worthy citizens, obviously anxious to please and be pleased. (She was including among them David Jasper, if not exactly tolerant and benign at least familiar to the scene, knowing what to expect and mainly accepting it.)

She ushered them in, and Mr. Chester introduced her. There was one colonel, two knights, two ministers, one of religion and one of politics, some doctors – but not of medicine, she gathered, Doctor David and several Misters, of which Mr. Snedley was one.

She stood politely awaiting their wishes, and all at once she was Catriona, ten years old again, anticipating a lollipop out of the pocket of that plump gentleman with the white thatch ... a string of beads or a charm from that other twinkling-eyed old man. The rest would ruffle her hair, pick her up for a kiss and she would rub the kiss off afterwards where the moustache had tickled. There had been one Board member she had particularly loved, who gave her rides on his feet. Doctor David ... how would she have considered him at ten years old?

'Sister by right, or is it just a courtesy title?' asked Mr. Snedley, and Catriona grew up ten years.

'I'm certificated, sir,' she answered, for ... going briefly back to ten ... that was how you answered the Mr. Snedley type of men, you said: 'Sir.'

'Humph,' Mr. Snedley said. He looked at the flowers. 'Not healthy, surely?'

'They're removed at night, sir.'

'All these books—'

'Most of the children are keen readers, sir.'

'But not at night-time when they should be asleep, when lights should be out. On that subject, Morrison' ... he addressed Colonel Morrison ... 'did you see the electricity bill? Shocking! Absolutely out of proportion.' Mr. Snedley looked at the books on the cupboard tops as though he now knew why.

'Lights are out at—' began Catty.

'What are these toys doing on the beds?'

'It's ... it's just a touch,' Catty stammered. 'Put like that over their night attire, it—'

'So many toys,' tch-tched Mr. Snedley. 'More than my own family ever had, I'm sure.'

Catty was sure, too. She had categorized Mr. Snedley at once. He might be rich, but he possessed that most undesirable trait in a rich person – the miser touch. Even though what was spent in Camp Universe could not personally affect him, since he was a Board member and a contributor he suffered from a compulsion to feel that it did, he resented every penny spent.

Horrified, she heard her own voice answering Mr. Snedley: 'Why shouldn't they have these things? Why should they have less? With the exception of Mardi, who is only on loan while her parents recover from an accident, they are either the child of a deserted parent, or a neglected child, or an unwanted child, but they are not, and have not been, and judging by their behaviour here, for I've watched carefully, never will be delinquent, they have no blemish, there's no mark of wrongdoing or misbehaviour against them, so why should they be underprivileged?' She added: 'Sir.'

She did not mean it impertinently, but she knew wretchedly as she tacked that final Sir to her answer that it sounded like that.

Mr. Snedley turned a bleak grey and said thinly: 'It costs a considerable amount to maintain a child, Sister Quentin. I should know. I have a family.'

'And the means to give them everything, I should think, not that little less.'

'I have reared my family to expect only that little less. I pride myself that my tight management has had results.'

'What kind of results?' Catty was horrified to hear her voice again, this time without the Sir.

'Unpampered children for one thing.' Mr. Snedley was losing his temper. 'I admit that prior to this present inspection, in the boys' section to be explicit, I was not quite satisfied, I admit that I saw a need for tighter management, the management I availed my family, and I, mark you, was in a vastly different position.'

'Yes, we know that you're rich,' Catty actually said.

'I admit,' continued Mr. Snedley, ignoring Catty's insertion, 'that I thought then that not only should expenses be covered but with a closer financial watch even a little profit showed.'

'Profit!' came in Catty, aghast. 'But, sir, here is your profit, these children are your profit.'

'But this,' went on Mr. Snedley, losing his bleak grey now and becoming a dull red, 'is the final argument against the sort of charity this place is running.'

'We never call it charity,' Mr. Chester came in, and he was a bright, not a dull, red.

'Folly, then? Or has it reached disaster? Have the books—'

'No.' It was David Jasper, and he stepped forward. 'The books have not balanced. They didn't in Our Founder's day with twelve wards, so how could they with four times that number?'

'The existing number should never have been accepted,' blazed Mr. Snedley. 'Can you give me one reason why they were accepted?'

'Because, sir, they were there. Because the twelve grew up and became twenty-four, thirty-six, forty-eight. I don't mean that literally, of course, but I do mean there are now many more children, and will be more. The only way to "profit", as you put it, is to cut out the supply of wards so that the demand they make leaves room for the balance you feel we should make.'

'Not just I, Doctor Jasper, others. Several of us here are businessmen. We know you can't run on a loss. Carter? Brentwood?' He looked around.

There was a silence.

'Well,' said Mr. Snedley furiously, 'are you leaving it all to me? You can, you know, there's nothing to make you back me up, *but can you function without what I donate?* Think that out.'

'It's not entirely as one-sided as you express it, Snedley,' said one of the men whom Catty sorted out as either Carter or Brentwood – anyway, one of the business tycoons. 'As with us, it's not entirely unprofitable for you to make Camp Universe your interest.'

'You mean they have to be supplied with certain

things,' said Mr. Snedley. 'Well, *you* supply them yourself.'

'I said so.'

'And at a lower rate than to other customers.'

'But still it's a profitable rate and a sure market.'

'This is abominable! I make a fair criticism and I'm victimized!' snorted Mr. Snedley.

'It was not a fair criticism and you are not victimized, you are only not agreed with, Mr. Snedley.' It was David Jasper again.

'Oh, I know by the rest, they're not commercial men, but you, Mr. Carter, and—'

'No,' said Mr. Carter, and Mr. Brentwood added to that.

'Then see if you still say so when I withdraw,' burst out Mr. Snedley.

'Your trade with Universe, too?' asked David. 'Groceries, isn't it?'

Mr. Snedley ignored him. 'See how you function then!' he tossed.

The Colonel came in calmly. 'It would mean more from each of us, admittedly, but distributed around I think we could do just that, Mr. Snedley, function without you. Gentlemen?' He glanced round the other members and one by one they nodded.

'You . . . you . . .' Mr. Snedley's last 'you' was at Catty, and she actually withdrew a pace. Withdrew into arms that held her firmly from the back so that no one would have noticed them there, so that only she was aware, that straightened her, that braced her, that still stopped there after Mr. Snedley had stamped out and across to his car, followed by a distinctly jaunty body of men ushered across to Horizon Hall for tea and jubilation . . . for judging by the smiles it was jubilation . . . by Mr. Chester.

Still she was held in David's arms.

He took a long time to release her, and before he did he turned her round to him. She saw that he was laughing.

'Scared you, didn't he?'

'A little,' she admitted.

'You should have known that I was here.'

But I knew it, she thought, I always know it. Sometimes I wish I didn't because I can't understand my awareness, I mean I know as my employer ... well, employer in a way ... I should be conscious of you, but it isn't only like that, it's—

'Yes, Sister?' He was looking at her closely, and she forced herself to answer rationally.

'I didn't know what to expect. I – I had spoken out of turn.'

'You never spoke better words, they rang like Te Deums in my ear. That fellow has been a thorn in the Board's side from the moment he became a member, for the distinct purpose – yes, I'm going to say it, of ridding himself of some of his surplus stock. We have other commercial men, but they are entirely different. I tell you, House-mother, you've done a very good deed today. Were you the little ward that you looked when the Board entered, I'd reward you now with a lollipop, or a doll or – What other rewards did a girl orphan receive?'

'Tosses in the air. Kisses,' she said unthinking.

'Can I choose?' Without waiting for her to answer, he leaned down and kissed her. A light kiss ... but not one to be rubbed off, even if there had been a moustache.

'I'm not ten years old now,' she said a little indistinctly.

'No,' he said, and paused. 'I was aware of that.'

What she would have answered she did not know. Whether he would have gone on, she did not know. And was not to know, for Mrs. Chester bustled in, a smile from ear to ear.

'This is really good news! That man out of our hair at last! And the credit is to you, dear. You're wanted in the Hall. There's not a member not waiting to shake your hand.'

'And toss you in the air, kiss you,' said David Jasper softly to Catty.

'What's that, Doctor?' asked Mrs. Chester.

'I said rule me out, Mrs. C. I'm in the middle of my rounds, I only sandwiched in this visit because Snedley was coming.'

'He won't be coming any more,' rejoiced Mrs. Chester, and David Jasper joined in the rejoicing.

But, as he had said, he did not join in the jubilations in Horizon hall. Over tea and cake the members beamed at Catty and assured her that she had said what they all had longed to say ever since Snedley's acceptance into the Universe Committee. She was patted and petted, and really it was not so much different from ten years ago.

Tony, also purring over the news, asked if they could now go ahead with the Open Day and Fête that had been proposed and promptly rejected by Mr. Snedley as an unwarranted expense.

'Perhaps we don't make as much out of it as we should,' Tony said, 'but the public sees how we function.'

'By all means go ahead,' said the Board.

After they had gone, farewelled by Catty who returned their waves ... and a blown kiss from one old dear ... Tony walked beside Catty back to Sky House.

'I felt very strongly about the Open Day Fête,' he told her. 'A place like this must be seen and heard.'

'Tell me what you had in mind, Tony?'

'Visitors to be conducted around our different activities ... on family days the kids just stop with their parents or what-have-yous.'

'Yes?'

'Also, the sale of some of our wares. The boys' carpentry, for instance, basket-making.'

'You could put some of your own oranges in the baskets.'

'You've caught on, Catriona.'

'But the Board vetoed it?'

'One did, and that was enough. Snedley was so unpleasant, it simply wasn't worth fighting him. But someone did today. You deserve a reward, Catriona.'

'I got it.' She said it before she thought, then laughed

135

self-consciously. 'I mean I got it when that man walked out of Sky House.'

'If I had been there I would have cheered. But on to my plan. Would you be in it?'

'In what way?'

'Tours of your part of Universe. Handicraft, if any. A stall selling things. Display of activities.'

'Of course.' Already she was caught up with enthusiasm. 'I could have Anne in her nurse's uniform taking groups through the hospital. Then three of the others have been making felt animals. We've been trying out sweets, too ... you know, Tony, those uncooked fridge ones. Then some of the girls might like to run a wishing well, a lucky dip, a—'

'You've got it!' Tony beamed.

From that moment on there was not an idle hour. Sky House threw itself into the preparations with such enthusiasm that sometimes Catty laughingly had to call a halt.

She had allowed the girls to choose what they wanted to do, and instinctively they had gone to what was closest to them. For example, Adrienne and Jean were making designs for a floral carpet. Nora and Clare were planning a baby stall, with knitted toys as well as bibs and bootees offering. The lucky dip was in the happy hands of a trio of the gayer girls. The sweets ... being practised now ... were to be handed over to the customers in small raffia baskets made by the hobby group.

Catty was rehearsing Gloria, who had a decided dramatic bend, to tell fortunes in the sand. She had taken out a sari she had bought on her way out and decided that, concealingly draped, it would give Gloria the right mystic air.

There was to be folk-dancing between the boys' gym display, and that took up more of Catty's time. Several of the better swimmers would perform a water ballet.

The waitresses would be needed for teas in Horizon Hall, and Anne, of course, would be the queen ... or should it be Florence Nightingale? ... of the hospital. Anne, even though Gloria's sari looked very glamorous, was rapturous over her role ... even to the extent of saying once to Catty: 'I think when my mother sees me, Sister Pussycat, she might – she might—'

Catty said warmly, 'Darling, I'm sure she will.'

Tony meanwhile was even busier than Catty. From across the hill wafted the sound of his band, the skirl of his pipes, the tramp of his marching squad. He was rehearsing athletic displays, boxing, wrestling, self-defence. He was arranging guided tours of the orchard, piggery, poultry runs, the different workshops. He was running an orange juice stall.

'All we need now,' he said exhaustedly on the Friday before the Fête, 'is fine weather.'

'Sky House is praying for it,' Catty confided.

She must have been depleted, for she did not wake up to see if the prayers had been answered until she was roused by the girls. They tapped politely at first, and then, in mounting excitement, in an urgent tattoo. 'Sister Pussycat, it's beautiful, it's just the Day!'

Jumping up and going to the window, Catty saw that it was.

Even this early it was not merely a promise of a beautiful day, it was already a glorious fulfilment. There was a phosphorescent sheen in the eastern sky, but you knew that the blue and the golden in it would win, and even as Catty watched it did. Gold buttered the slats of the blind, blue became entangled in the lace of the curtains. The gentlest of morning breezes stirred both.

'Oh, hurry up, Sister,' her girls entreated.

They did not bother going over to Horizon Hall for breakfast, milk from the house fridge and cookies was all they wanted, and though it was not a balanced beginning, and probably Doctor Jasper would have frowned, Catty did not think it would hurt for once. Indeed, she doubted if any of the girls could have eaten more, and knowing fêtes, perhaps it was just as well to leave space for the many goodies that were sure to be offered.

Dressing the girls took some time. The waitresses, the stallholders, the display young women. Anne. Today Anne had to be the *perfect* nurse, and she certainly was.

'You squeak,' said Ann Mary of the starched skirts, 'and your pinny is white like snow.'

'That's how it should be,' said Anne, looking proudly at herself in the mirror, starting at the peaked cap and going slowly down to the feet in the polished shoes.

Gloria was enfolded in the mysterious sari, then hurriedly Catty put on a floral shift and matching sandals, then established the girls in their chosen positions, for the Fête was an all-day one, and the ten o'clock bus should bring the first contingent of customers.

Promptly at ten it did, and as they poured out, Ben, the driver, told Tony and Catty the good news that an extra bus would be along behind him as there had been more visitors than he could cope with.

'It looks like a bumper day,' he said. 'Have you seen the car park? It's filled already.'

But this made no difference to the big showy model that came in last but still snitched a key position. So, thought Catty bleakly, watching Anne's mother get out and evidently promise the flashy man behind the wheel that she would not be long. Harry was still on the scene. She realized she was shaking slightly, and instinctively looked around for David Jasper, who would be sure to be somewhere among the throng. She could not see him.

Resolutely, telling herself she was being a timid character, she did the rounds of her girls. They were all performing their duties most creditably. The sweets stall was doing a fine trade, mother-to-be and grandmas-to-be were exclaiming with delight over the baby stall wares, the lucky dips were crowded with eager dippers.

She crossed to the dancing displays that were being sandwiched between the boys' band offerings and physical exercises and found that they were performing excellently.

The tea staff was receiving praise for its quick service, so there was no more to be checked except the sand-divining tent and the hospital bay open for inspection.

Catty went in first to peep at Gloria. The young seer was in her element, she had a distinct flair, Catty thought. She had taught her a few stock phrases to intone, such as: 'Circumstances will take place that will change your future' ... 'You are about to travel to far places.' But Gloria, she saw, did not need them, she had a quick wit and could make up words of her own. 'There is sunshine on your path,' she was whispering huskily in a voice that sounded so seer-like that Catty caught her breath in admiration and intrigue, 'but the sand also tells me there are some shadows. – Ah, what is this?'

'What is it?' said the fortune-seeker eagerly.

'A sand sign that says you will receive an offer that will take you by surprise.' She was using one of the stock phrases now.

'It'll be Jack,' said the fortune-seeker happily. 'Any more?'

Gloria had seen Catty, and she intoned, also from her conned text: 'Your road is about to be crossed by a person of the medical profession.'

'Ooh,' said the seeker, 'that would be Doctor Brown. You *are* good!' She gave Gloria an extra coin, and the girl, after she had departed, looked up at Catty and giggled.

'That last was for you, Sister. Doctor David came looking for you.'

'How are you doing, dear?'

'You just heard,' smiled Gloria confidently. To someone standing at the flap of the tent she called, 'Come in, please,' and a woman did. It was Anne's mother. But Anne's mother did not sit down on the floor beside the sand as Gloria told her. She had recognized Catty, and she stood and looked at her instead.

'Oh, our house-mother,' she said.

'Yes, Mrs. Meekes.'

'And where's that daughter of mine? I see, anyway, you haven't got her waiting on table. At some stall, I suppose, serving. She wouldn't be in any dancing, she's as clumsy as an elephant. Why couldn't she be here? Quite an attractive get-up, I must say. But I suppose the fancy dress is reserved for your pets.'

Catty said as steadily as she could, 'Gloria happened to have a flair for acting.'

'Even if my girl had you would still have other ideas,' suggested Anne's mother, taking out her cigarettes.

Catty forbore to tell her that a small tent was not the place to smoke. She said, 'Would you like to go across to Anne?'

'After I'm done here, I'm not throwing fifty cents away. What have you got to tell me?' The last to a frankly unhappy Gloria.

But the child was a good actress, and she saw it through. She trotted out all the stock phrases, to which Anne's mother snorted when she had done: 'Cheap at half the price.' She got up, lit another cigarette and strolled out of the tent. Catty followed her.

'Anne—' Catty began.

'Oh, she'll keep. I'm going to have a cup of tea first.' She started off, then stopped abruptly. 'She's not waitressing, I looked in as soon as I came. Where is she, then? Not doing the washing up, I hope?'

'Something that will really make you proud, Mrs. Meekes. Anne is conducting the tours of the hospital.'

'Oh, yes?'

'As nurse.'

'In another word, slushy,' nodded Mrs. Meekes.

'As nurse,' repeated Catty. 'And on that subject . . .' Impulsively she burst out all the things she had to say about Anne and Anne's ambition, how lots of nurses were trained for the career, but only a few were born for it, and how Anne . . . how Anne . . . She said it more eagerly than wisely, she knew that, but she felt so strongly for the girl, she was so anxious, she simply let the words flow out.

Flow, that is, until a hard wall dammed them.

'Finished?' drawled Mrs. Meekes.

'Y-yes.'

'Then let me put in a few words. Nursing to me is the same as what you had her in before. You're determined to make a domestic of her, aren't you, and though it's probably all she's good for, she's not going to be. See? She's nearly fifteen. Time she earned something.'

'She can't start work yet,' came in Catty desperately, 'she's under school leaving age.'

'Oh, yes, she can work. You can get special permission to take them away from school if you're left destitute, like I was.' Catty could not help glancing down at the expensive dress Mrs. Meekes wore . . . but wore like a rag.

'Nurse!' she sneered next. 'Fetch me this, fetch me that, but put me in an apron and call me Nurse and everything's rosy. But it's not going to be. I'll take Anne away next month. She'll be of age then. I'll see the Department and explain my case.' – Again Catty glanced at the expensive clothes.

Desperately she suggested, 'Then if you do, I know that she would be accepted as an aide, Mrs. Meekes. They take them from the age of—'

'Aide? You mean . . . yes, I believe you do. Stubborn, aren't you? Well, she's not going to be. There's lots of jobs for a strong fifteen-year-old. Or come to think of it I might even keep her home to help me. As Harry always says, I do far too much.'

'Mrs. Meekes—'

'Yes?' Anne's mother looked hard at Catty, and Catty lost her courage.

'Nothing,' she stammered, 'nothing . . . except won't you just go over and see her?' If she saw her daughter, she thought, if she just saw her, so trim, so straight, so white, so starched and – and so sweet.

'No, I haven't time. Harry must be chewing his nails to the quicks waiting for me. But you can give her my message. She's leaving next month. And there won't be any of this silly business, either. She'll do what I say and go where I tell her. Just prime her up about that.' She wheeled round and went towards the tea hall, but half-way there Harry must have seen her and put his fat thumb on the loud fancy horn, and, laughing, she turned and went to the ornate car instead. It revved up and the next moment was speeding down the drive.

Mechanically Catty crossed to the hospital.

Anne had just finished showing a group through, and was waiting to show another group.

'Did you see your mother, Anne?'

'I saw the car. Is – is she coming over?'

'She had to leave in a hurry.' Catty paused. 'She said to tell you so.' Miserably she tacked that on.

'Oh, yes,' accepted Anne. Then she asked tentatively, 'Did she say anything else?'

'No, I don't believe so. Were – were you expecting her to?'

'I thought she might have something to say about – about me doing this.' Anne glanced down at her uniform, and something in her suddenly defeated stance stirred Catty.

'But she did. She seemed pleased ... you know, darling, a kind of surprised and proud of you at the same time.'

'*Mother?*'

'Yes. I – I expect she never thought you had it in you.'

'No, she wouldn't think I had. But *pleased*, Sister? Surprised, you said, and she would be. But *proud*?' There was disbelief in Anne's voice ... but withal a faint urgent hope.

'Yes, darling. She was really amazed, and – and – Well, as I said, she was proud.'

'Mother was proud?'

'Yes.'

'She'll be prouder later on,' Anne resolved.

'I know she will, Anne.'

'She has always said I'd have to leave when I could

142

earn something. I could be an aide, you know, until I became a student. You don't get much, but if Mother feels like that—'

'There's another party waiting to look over your hospital, Nurse Anne,' said Catty formally, and she stepped aside for the group waiting at the door.

'This way, please,' she heard Anne intone. 'Now, this is our isolation ward, and in here . . .'

Catty went outside. There was noise and movement everywhere, but somehow she felt she was standing alone.

Not alone, though. David Jasper joined her. 'I've been looking for you, Sister,' he said.

'Yes, Gloria . . . the seer . . . told me.'

'Read it in the sand, did she?' he smiled. 'It was just to warn you that the Meekes woman was here, and that if you needed me I'd come. I doubt if she'd start anything with me around.'

'She's gone,' said Catty dully.

He looked across at the parking area, at the space empty now from the ornate car, and nodded.

'Did she start anything?' he asked.

'Yes.'

'Was it Anne?'

'Yes.'

'Did she go and see her?'

'No.'

'Left a message, then?'

'Yes.'

'How did our nurse take it?'

'She was pleased, she was lit up.'

'What, Sister?'

'I didn't tell her.' Catty was so near to tears she knew at any moment she would be unable to hold them back.

What he had done once before, and it had been because of Anne then, he did again now. He stepped in front of her and stopped there until she gained control.

'What is it?' he said quietly.

'I told her something else.'

'You white-lied, you mean?'

'Yes.'

There was a long pause. In that time Catty dried her eyes, blew her nose, straightened her dress, adjusted a strand of hair.

'I do myself,' said David Jasper, and putting his fingers under her elbow he guided her across for tea.

'Sister Pussycat,' whispered waitress Susan when they were seated, 'I've sneaked you the best cake, it's a cream puff.'

'And a lot of sugars,' said Ann Mary, who had the job of carrying around the sugar cubes. She busily plopped seven in Catty's cup, craftily telling her that she had been told only to give out two.

David Jasper protected his before he could be similarly favoured, and across the table they looked at each other and laughed.

'You did the right thing,' he said, and as he took a cake, Susan watching to see he did not take Sister Pussycat's special cake that she had sneaked across, his big firm hand brushed hers.

Drinking the tea and not tasting the seven lumps, she who took no sugar, Catty still felt the brush of that hand against hers.

CHAPTER EIGHT

AND they *did* make a profit.

Tony, who had appealed to the Board: 'Perhaps we don't make as much out of it as we should, but the public sees how we function,' was dumbfounded with disbelief. But when words could come, he hugged Catty instead. David Jasper, coming into the scene, drawled: 'It should be moonlight, and by the orange grove, Williams. Our house-mother likes the right setting.'

Catty was annoyed but Tony only grinned and said, 'I'll try that, too.'

The takings proved so substantial that a Universe holiday comp became a fact instead of a dream.

'A holiday camp!' Catty had looked around her when Tony and David had reported Universe's next move following the successful fête. There was everything for a holiday here, she claimed.

'But no sea,' Tony reminded her. He told Catty how a surfside villa called Blue Peter up at Rainbow Bay on the north coast had been bequeathed to Universe by a departed supporter, but how up till now there had been insufficient means to furnish it as would be necessary for a family of twenty or thirty instead of the customary five, six or so.

'There's plenty of verandahs,' gloated Tony, 'so all we need are beds.'

'Don't you eat?' asked Catty pointedly.

'Alfresco,' planned Tony. 'Perhaps, in case of bad weather, we could splash out on a big table.'

'Chairs on which to sit at the table.'

'Benches would be better.'

He showed Catty the plan of the house, and how, thanks to the fête, it could function at last. There was not a fortune to spend on it, but on the other hand there was not a great deal on which to be spent.

They reduced it at last to beds and what went with them, the large table and benches and a new bigger range. Universe could supply the culinary needs from its own ample store, Tony would shop around for discount cots and mattresses, and the job of buying the linen and spreads was given to Catty.

Ann Mary had not attended school all the week, following a tummy upset – the result, Catty suspected, of sampling more of the sugar cubes that as sugar girl she had been entrusted with than she had doled out.

Doctor David had ordered a few days in bed, and Catty had nursed and petted her, receiving in return Ann Mary's fond accounts of the grandmother whose face Catty had. – 'Yes, darling,' said Catty faintly.

She in her turn talked about Gaby and Georgie, not noticing in her wistfulness the pique in Ann Mary until the little girl said as she had before: 'I don't like those kids.'

'But you would, Ann Mary. See, here they are.' She showed the smallest one her small ones, her Roger's babies.

Ann Mary said nothing.

Now that the little girl was up again, Catty decided she would take her down to Penrith for a treat after her days in bed while she selected the linen and spreads for the holiday house.

She had been provided with an order for the same firm as before, but this time there was no doctor to drive them down, they took the house bus to Emu Heights then the train instead.

It was while she was buying the train tickets that Catty noticed something different about her handbag, but Ann Mary called just then that the train was coming, and she forgot about it.

She never thought about it either at Penrith, which was definitely her idea of a pleasing country town with its long meandering main street instead of a busy square, for the purchases took up her attention . . . she decided finally on checked linen, on tangerine spreads . . . and after that there was the pleasant preoccupation of lunch.

Nor did she think on the journey back.

But, cleaning out her handbag at Sky House, once more the difference in its interior struck her, and she looked closer and saw that her leather folder of photos was missing.

She searched her room. It was a smooth leather case and easily could have slipped out. Unsuccessful, she went across to the house bus, checked where she had sat, checked the rest of the seats, then asked Ben who had driven the bus down to Emu Heights station. He had seen no case.

'Perhaps you lost it in the train, Sister.'

'No.' It was as she had paid for the tickets that she had noticed that the bag seemed different. 'It's not money,' she assured the concerned Ben, then went back to Sky House *very* concerned herself.

For it was Ann Mary, of course. The smallest one had removed the folder of 'those kids', and how could she blame her? The little hungry heart that had found in Catty the grandmother who loved her, possibly the only one who did love her, had resented those two small people whom Catty loved. Too late Catty realized she had made too much of them to Ann Mary.

She would have preferred to have dropped the subject, reassured an unsure child with her love for *her*, but she wanted the photos back if the photos were still intact. She doubted it.

She doubted it more when Ann Mary, questioned gently, went pale, then red, then burst into tears. Alas, Catty knew Ann Mary's tears, they finished in sobs, sobs that went on for hours, so she patted the smallest one's head, said it didn't matter, and tried to tell herself she didn't need the photos, anyway, they were in her heart.

But she must have looked tired . . . or something . . . that night, for when David Jasper came to read Chapter

Thirteen he asked her if anything was wrong. Not only did he ask it, he looked it, his glance was deep and probing. He even seemed disturbed himself.

'Nothing,' she lied. 'It was rather a long day. I chose striped sheets, I thought they would be more "holiday", also easier to launder if there was no machine, and tangerine covers. Orange is bright, don't you think?'

'Bright,' he said, still staring at her.

It had been decided that the boys, with Tony, should enjoy the first sea break, then anything missing for comfort could be added before the girls, with Catty, took their holiday. Mr. and Mrs. Chester would go with Catty, even though she insisted she would be all right.

It was strange without the boys' company. Even though they only met up at meals, swimming, occasional games, even though they were on the other side of the hill, the camp was different without them.

Catty, still depressed over the photo wallet, might have been more in the dumps without Tony's company, for Tony was good company, but the departure of Mardi took her mind off herself. For Mardi's parents, accident victims, were better at last, and Mardi was to go home.

It was while she was saying goodbye that Catty remembered Mr. Snedley, and she wished ... angrily ... that she had him here now.

'So many toys,' he had said. 'More than my own family ever had.'

Yes, Mr. Snedley, but they had their family. Look around you, Mr. Snedley, see the other faces, the hungry, desperate faces, the faces of children who want to go home, too. *Look*, Mr. Snedley. Who is underprivileged now?

'Goodbye, Sister. Goodbye, kids.' With a quick wave, for with her arm around her mother ... the other round her father ... she did not want to waste time, not after all this time, on other things, Mardi was gone.

Silently Catty led her group back to Sky House. She let them stay up longer that night. Her God Bless was very tender.

Mr. Chester told her the next day that she would have a replacement. 'There's a waiting list, Sister Quentin. The Child Welfare are sending along a Gwendolen Grace.'

'A loner?' Catty almost hoped she was an orphan, or at least orphaned on one side; it was the divided ones that she found the hardest to bear.

'Both parents,' said Mr. Chester. He added: 'And a family. Two brothers and a sister, in fact.'

'Then—?'

'She has been in a corrective school,' Mr. Chester said unhappily. Although the Camp manager, and only responsible for the mechanics and not the soul, he was a very sensitive man.

'Has she got a bad history?'

'More a frequent one, Sister.'

'What – theft?'

'No, general mischief. In short, a difficult child.' He was thoughtful a while, then went on, 'The father is a distinguished scientist, the mother no less successful in her field. The other three children, two younger than Gwendolen, are quite exceptionally bright.'

'Gwendolen is not?'

'Well, she isn't dull,' said Mr. Chester, scratching his head. 'The report simply says it's hard to establish anything except waywardness.'

'Prompted, perhaps, by brilliance all around her,' said Catty sympathetically.

'That makes sense, but the family background doesn't. They're kind and loving.'

'So much so that they've given her up?'

'The last naughtiness had to be handled by the police and welfare, the parents had the matter taken right away from them. But they moved mountains to get Gwendolen out of the corrective place to Universe. So, Sister, I don't think you can put the blame there.'

'Perhaps unwittingly—' murmured Catty, but she let

the matter rest. Mr. Chester had enough on his mind dealing with the grocery and fuel lists.

Gwendolen arrived the next day, sulky and introverted, rather as Catty had anticipated. Catty was glad that the female side of Universe was to leave for a short break at Rainbow Bay at the end of the week. In a place that was new to the others as well as herself, Gwendolen might relax more and be less the little mollusc in a shell.

She suggested a small brown snail. Rather immature for her thirteen years, nothing special in colouring, one could almost see protective antennae rising out of her cap-cropped hair, ready to tell her when to withdraw. And they seemed to tell her often. After three days Catty had not held any conversation with Gwendolen, and she doubted if any of the others had reached her, either. On the other hand she was certainly not naughty.

The boys arrived home from Rainbow Bay bleached of hair and brown of limb. Tony reported that the beach house was really a beach house. You could almost roll on to the sand from your bed. When Catty looked alarmed he reminded her that all the girls could swim, even the smallest could keep herself up.

'But the surf is different.'

'Actually although it's the coast, there's not much surf. There's a reef farther out and it breaks down the rollers to pleasant ripples – so much so that we did more sailing than surfing.'

'Is there a boat?'

'A nicely manageable one. Oh, yes, you'll enjoy yourself.'

The night before their departure, it seemed they wouldn't enjoy themselves, for it seemed they wouldn't go. Mr. and Mrs. Chester received a call to say that an overseas relation was spending the week in Sydney, and though Mrs. Chester said she wouldn't dream of disappointing the girls, and though Mr. Chester said a man was a necessary item in a house and he wouldn't think of letting them down, it was obvious that the pair of them were anxious to entertain their relative together.

'We'll postpone Rainbow Bay.' Catty was disappointed herself, for as well as looking forward to the break, she was looking forward to getting somewhere with Gwendolen. It mightn't work, but at least she wanted to try.

'But of course you won't postpone it,' said Tony later, Tony who understood from his own young gang how let down children can be. 'Mrs. Chester you can do without, she's a good soul but not essential if you're there. But I agree with Mr. Chester that a man is needed, for the fuel stove alone. Wood has to be chopped.'

'I could do it,' offered Catty.

'And chop off your toe,' said Tony cheerfully. 'No, Catriona, a man, not a girl, to play head of the house.'

'All right then, but produced from where? You can't leave the boys, not with the C's not in attendance.'

'Leave it to Uncle Tony,' he grinned.

It was soon afterwards that Bevan rang. He was so enthusiastic, so eager to have a few days at Rainbow Bay that it seemed redundant to thank him.

But several days ... They were to be there for a week.

'David Jasper has agreed to go the other time,' Tony said.

Catty replied, 'I see.'

They went down in the Camp bus to Emu Heights station the next morning, caught a train to Sydney, then without leaving Central a train up to Rainbow Bay.

It was all new to Catty, and she watched as eagerly as any of her wards the passing scene. First Sydney's inner suburbs, then over the green Parramatta River to higher, more leisurely towns. After that, rural settings like their own Emu Heights, cultivated acres, timbered hills, but always not far away the sea.

They alighted at a sleepy station serving a dreaming little town, consisting of a church, a handful of shops and a bus marked Rainbow Bay. Bevan, who was travelling by car, and who had been disappointed because Catty could not travel with him, arrived almost at the same time and succeeded in persuading Catty to finish the journey in comfort.

'The bus looks comfortable,' she said.

'There's no cushions. I brought one especially, Catriona.'

'You think of everything,' she laughed.

'Not really. Just one thing. One possibility.'

'Anne,' called Catty crisply, 'I'll be travelling ahead with Mr. Bruce to open up. You're responsible for the girls.' She knew she could trust Anne.

They drove through eucalyptus bush for some miles, the bus panting ponderously a few bends behind them, then all at once a flag-blue sea almost accosted them with its glitter. There was a long golden beach with a small cove at one end which would be Rainbow Bay.

Blue Peter proved quite a substantial house. It had evidently been built for holiday requirements. There were wide verandahs all round with rooms leading on to them. There was a large bathroom with double everything, and the kitchen was ample enough to cater for the entire party should the weather be inclement and alfresco meals not practicable.

Catty set the girls making their beds, then she said what they were waiting for, that they could get into their swimming things and run down to the water. While they were exploring the rocks, building castles, taking cautious dips, for the day's sun was nearly over and the sea growing chilly, Catty and Bevan went across to the one shop to supplement what they had brought from Universe.

The varied stock amused Catty, but she supposed one store would have to carry everything. Huddled together were bacon rashers, tinned jam, magazines, dolls and friction cars, check shirts and sun-hats.

'I have everything but glass eyes,' said the proud proprietor.

'One thing he does have is stale bullseyes,' said Bevan ruefully as they emerged, one of his cheeks bulged out.

Catty laughed and excused Mr. Jones. It would be hard, she said, to keep everything fresh in a place like this.

'I only hope the breeze keeps fresh, Catriona, I want to take the boat out. Can you sail?'

'No.'

'Neither can I, so we'll have fun.'

The next day was perfect, and not only Bevan and Catty sailed, but, in groups, all the girls. Bevan was very patient, and if their forward drives ... Bevan said he believed they were called that ... were not the crashing, smashing feats a boat should perform, if their fencing with sheet and tiller to parry each thrust and lunge of the wind and water was unspectacular, at least they had fun. Bevan was fun. Bevan ... Bevan was sweet.

'It says in my book,' he called to Catty, 'that this is sailing downhill.'

'Should downhill be such hard work?' Catty panted.

He was the best of company, and on the final night of his stop he proposed to Catty. He was everything she could ask, she liked him as much as she could like anybody, and wasn't it true that liking a person was more important ... well, *lasting*, anyway ... than loving them? Also she adored his grove, his background. In fact there was nothing she didn't like, so why ... why ...

'I'm sorry, Bevan,' she sighed.

'I didn't mean to rush you again, Catriona, it's just that I can't *not* move. You see my point?'

'No.'

'Then that's something, anyway,' he said cryptically.

He went early the next day. Oranges had to be tended. David Jasper would arrive that night.

Although the hours had been pleasantly filled at Rainbow Bay, Catty had found opportunity to observe Gwendolen. But she had got no further with her. The new background, new to the others as well, had not relaxed her, she was the same introverted little mollusc as before. This was going to be hard, Catty knew.

They spent the day on the beach again, one thing with sand and sea there was no entertainment worry. But when Ann Mary returned from a washed-up cask she had been examining, Catty saw that there was going to be a cleansing worry. The smallest girl had literally smothered herself with black grease.

'Into the tub with you, Ann Mary,' she called. The house had several old-fashioned baths, and certainly Ann Mary would need a high tide of hot water. 'No, no use to try to wash in the waves, you'll need a scrubbing brush and soap.'

Ann Mary was naturally not pleased, but when Catty produced some of her floating things, which, with an emergency like this in mind, she had wisely packed, she became more amiable. Catty got rid of the grease, then let the little girl play in the warm water.

Tea was always an early affair, for here appetites seemed to sharpen an hour before the customary time, so at five, Ann Mary still contentedly launching soap boats in the big old bath, Catty began preparations.

'What are we having, Sister Pussycat?' she called.

'Scrambled eggs, darling.' Scrambled eggs were a favourite with them all.

'Goody!' applauded the smallest girl. 'I'll get out.'

'Wait for me, Ann Mary, it's a big bath and a high climb.'

'I'll pull out the plug then.'

'Yes, pet.'

Catty heard the gurgle of the receding tide and knew that Ann Mary would be sitting fascinated as it left her high if not dry.

The next thing she heard was Ann Mary's scream.

Thinking the child had tried to climb out herself and had slipped, she ran to the bathroom. Ann Mary still sat where she had sat before, but she was in a panic and when she saw Catty she screamed again.

'I'm going down!' she cried.

'Oh, darling, don't be silly, you're too big.'

'I'm going, Sister Pussycat, my fingers have gone already!'

'Your fingers . . . oh, no!' For what seemed to happen always once in a child's life was now happening to Ann Mary. She had jammed her hand in the plughole. Three fat little fingers, fast growing fatter as almost visibly they swelled, were pushed through the holes in the steel strainer. Of course the water had not taken Ann Mary, she had put the fingers there herself, but this was no time to question or scold the child.

Catty's heart sank. If it had been anyone but Ann Mary! Sooner or later Ann Mary would start to cry, and then would come those big breathless enervating sobs.

Keeping as calm as she could, she knelt down and did the routine things. First of all an exploring finger to make sure the hand was trapped. It was. Next to see if the fingers would move. They wouldn't. Now Catty tried variation of water temperatures, tapping round the aperture, manipulation. All to no avail.

She knew what was really needed, and it was the assistance of a plumber. There would be no plumber at Rainbow Bay, but Mr. Jones might know where to get one. He might even be able to get the hand out himself.

The girls were coming up from the beach. Catty called as serenely as she could for Anne to come to her.

Anne, the little nurse, took it all in at once. 'I'll get Mr. Jones,' she said, and ran out. Thank heaven, appreciated Catty, for their eldest girl.

It was no use trying to vary the temperature, tap the aperture or manipulate any more, for Ann Mary shrank at any approach, that was all of Ann Mary except the entrapped hand. It appeared to be swelling.

Catty looked at her helplessly, hoping that Mr. Jones would shut his shop at once and run across, that he brought with him something to relieve the situation, but what, she did not know.

All this time Ann Mary had been protesting loudly it had been nerve-racking to listen to, but at least it was something that Catty could cope with. Then, just as she had dreaded, the cries turned to those enervating sobs of Ann Mary's, the sobs that racked her little body, tore at everyone who heard her.

'Oh, darling, don't,' appealed Catty, but the sobs rose higher.

All this time the girls had been watching silently, and Catty had been grateful for their quiet behaviour.

Then one of them came forward, and into the bath beside Ann Mary she placed the teddy bear that had travelled with the smallest one. The sobs lessened slightly as Ann Mary looked at Edward Bear.

Gwendolen ... for it was their new girl, Gwendolen Grace ... did not stop at that, she went out and came back with a kitten that had been befriended by the house, and especially by the youngest, and she put the kitten in the bath as well.

This time there was a definite pause in the sobs, and during the pause Gwendolen brought in the big dog who had been sitting on the mat when they had arrived, between whose paws the kitten slept when it was tired, and she put the dog in, too. The final offering was a tin of biscuits.

By now the bath was full of girl, bear, cat, dog and biscuits. But also the air was full of ordinary sounds again, not frenzied sobs. And wonder of wonders, without Ann Mary pulling and straining and forcing, the little fingers were quite visibly reducing their size.

'Petroleum jelly, soap,' said a voice beside the kneeling Catty, and Catty looked up with relief to see that David Jasper had arrived.

Ann was behind him, and she gasped, still out of breath, 'Doctor David was asking Mr. Jones the direction as I got to the store, Sister Pussycat. How is Ann Mary?'

'Ann Mary,' said Catty thankfully, 'is out.'

'And no worse, either,' said David, taking the little girl up in his arms and examining the fingers. 'A bruise, perhaps, but nothing more.' He put the child down, then said clearly and warmly, 'Thanks entirely to the one who thought of all that.' He pointed to the dog who rather liked the cool bath and had decided to sleep, the kitten already asleep between his paws, to the biscuits, to the bear.

'Gwendolen,' said Catty proudly, 'our new, very clever girl.' She brought Gwendolen to the fore.

'Clever isn't good enough,' said Doctor David. 'She's resourceful, which is much more. Do you know what that means, Gwendolen?'

'Sort of,' said Gwendolen shyly, but with a light in her that Catty had not seen before. She wasn't a little mollusc any more, she was an extremely pleased girl. The other girls were flocking around her, making her a queen. Ann Mary was claiming her, refusing to go to anyone else, fastening on to her as she used to fasten on to Catty.

'I think you've lost a devotee, Sister Quentin,' said David.

Thinking of her photo wallet that she felt sure Ann Mary had destroyed because she had been jealous, Catty sighed, 'I could have done with that loss before.'

'And why?' he asked at once, asked sharply.

She flushed and answered, 'No reason,' and turned away. She would not have him probing into her affairs.

He waited a while, then when he saw she was not going to elaborate, he asked her about Gwendolen and she told him the little that she knew.

'I think,' he said when she had finished, 'that that's all over.'

'I'd love to think so, but how could one situation change a child?'

'Not change the child, change the circumstances fretting and tormenting the child, making the child anti-social.'

'Mr. Chester said the family report was excellent.'

'He's right. I can vouch for that. I happen to know the Graces.'

'Then—?' She looked at him in bewilderment. If he agreed that Gwendolen's family was a good one, how could he speak as he just had, say that circumstances had made Gwendolen what she was?

'The Grace mother and father are exceptionally brilliant. I was at University with Hugo, and he took every prize. Gretel took them two years after.'

'Gretel is Mrs. Grace?'

'Yes.'

'If they were both so gifted,' said Catty with feeling, 'surely they could see there was something wrong with Gwendolen.'

'Nothing wrong, just so effortlessly brilliant as they were, and as the others were.'

'You mean the other children?'

'Yes.'

'But this is preposterous! Parents like the Graces should have seen it.'

'And would have had they had the chance. I feel sure of that. But gifts like the Grace gifts have demands made on them.'

'I should think the understanding of a child would be a bigger demand.'

'Yes, *you* would think that,' he said gently. 'But then' . . . before she could warm herself in that . . . 'did you ever major in psychology? In applied what-have-you? In ancient this-or-that? No, I thought not. There's only a nursing diploma on your wall.'

'It's not on the wall,' she said angrily. 'I'm sorry I disappoint you as regards brains, but after all, it was a nursing diploma that was requested, not a degree.'

'Calm down,' he advised. 'You're as emotional as Ann Mary.'

'I can promise you I won't burst into sobs.'

'Then that's something,' he shrugged. 'But before we leave the subject, Sister Quentin, I must remind you that I'm only a member of and not the entire Board. Also' . . . a pause . . . 'I wasn't disappointed.'

'That I can well believe. You'd hate to employ anyone whose brains matched yours.'

'This family who adopted a waif of ten,' he said, 'by the name of Catriona . . .'

'Yes?' She looked up sharply, wondering what he was going to probe now.

But there was no probing. He simply said hatefully, 'They never whacked you enough.'

'They never,' she answered, 'whacked at all.'

'As you just remarked, Sister, that I can well believe.'

'Tea!' called Anne from the big kitchen, and saying as coolly as she could, for she felt hot and annoyed, to David Jasper that it was only scrambled eggs and bread and honey, she led the way out.

Undoubtedly Ann Mary had transferred her adoration, and undoubtedly Gwendolen liked Ann Mary's love.

While Catty and Gwendolen stood on the beach the next day and David took the girls out, though in much more sergeant-major fashion than placid Bevan had afforded, the little mollusc came out of her shell.

'I have a younger sister and brother, but they're not like Ann Mary,' she said.

'You mean, Gwendolen, they don't run to you, depend on you. But perhaps they're older than our smallest.'

'Yes, they are, but they still never did. You see even though they're four and five years different from me, they're still cleverer than I am. They know the answers quicker. I know the answers in the end, but it takes time.'

'In lots of things you have to take time. Like in writing poetry, for instance. Or painting.'

'I like both of those,' admitted Gwendolen shyly, 'but my parents—'

'Would be terribly proud to have someone different, different from what they are and in what they do, what their other children are, and do. I don't think you've ever let them know, have you?'

'About poetry and painting and things? No.'

As Gwendolen stood silent after her admission, Catty said, 'You were very good yesterday with Ann Mary, Gwendolen.'

'But it wasn't clever, was it? Oh, I know you said it was, but it wasn't.'

'Doctor David said resourceful,' reminded Catty, 'and I agree. But I also think it was quite wonderful as well.'

'Wonderful? Me?'

'So much so that I'm going to write to your parents and tell them all about it. – You love your parents, don't you?'

'Yes, but they can't love me. I mean they're nice and they try, but how could they? I'm slow and I don't get prizes. I don't get things done.'

'So,' dared Catty, 'you've been trying to make them aware of you by doing things that ... well, things that you shouldn't.'

'Yes,' Gwendolen said.

'But you see now that there are different ways of showing them, and different ways of being clever. Would your sister, for instance ... what's her name, Gwendolen?'

'Frances.'

'Would Frances have thought to have calmed Ann Mary like that?'

'No,' admitted Gwendolen, 'but she's still a grade ahead of me in Maths, yet she's years younger.'

'Maths would never have saved Ann Mary.' – That was exaggerating, for Ann Mary's life had not been endangered, but still Catty went on. 'You have something intuitive in you, and by that, Gwendolen, I mean a sense of what to *do* and not just a sense of what can be done, that I believe they have not. Don't fret over grades and standards, darling. And don't try to make them aware of you by going on the way you have. Just act as you did yesterday, the quiet thoughtful way. Though' ... putting her arm around Gwendolen and *not* being repulsed ... 'I think you put those things in the bath very quickly.'

'I would have done it faster only ... well, I was afraid you'd say it was silly.'

'Never think like that, Gwendolen, just do.'

'But my mother and father—'

'They would be proud of you. Try it.'

Gwendolen did not answer for a while. Then she said, 'They're all coming up to see me on visiting day.'

'That will be nice.'

'Yes.'

'I'll talk to them,' said Catty. 'It will be about what I write in the letter. When they talk to you, you'll talk, too, won't you?'

There was a long pause, then Gwendolen said 'Yes' again.

The boat load came back, and Ann Mary, one of the crew, immediately claimed her new idol.

Watching the two girls running along the water's edge, David Jasper said, 'How does it feel to be disenthroned?'

'Oh, don't be silly!' She said it more sharply than she intended, but suddenly she was thinking of her precious photos that Ann Mary had removed because she was jealous, and now she was jealous no longer, but that didn't return Gaby and Georgie.

'Sister Pussycat,' came in his voice, 'I've spoken to you three times and you haven't answered.'

'Oh, I'm sorry. What was it, Doctor Jasper?'

'You're to come sailing with me, you're the only one left to go out.'

'I have been out with Bevan.'

He ignored that. He called, 'Anne, you're mother,' and turning back to the boat he nodded for Catty to come with him. After a moment's hesitation, she did.

Within minutes she knew that sailing with David was entirely different from sailing with Bevan. Bevan had taught the things he had read, like wetting your finger and holding it up to determine the wind direction, like twenty ways to get into trouble and twenty ways to get out . . . or so you hoped. It had been fun, but it had not been sea, sky, wind and a sailboat, the world of waters as it was with David.

They crossed out of Rainbow Bay, then blew down along the wide beach, sailing windward. Carefully David hoisted the mainsail into position and the canvas bellied out.

Had the leak occurred when they were rimming the beach they simply would have put in, but when Catty drew David's attention to the centre board that was showing water they had cleared the sands and were running into rocks.

He frowned, but nodded calmly, and tried working on the leak with matchsticks, some chewing gum that had been naughtily hidden by one of the 'sailors' under a seat and found triumphantly by Catty, finally with Catty's scarf. It was no good, the leak worsened.

'Can't we put back?' Catty shouted.

'We wouldn't make it. There's another small cove beyond the headland. I noticed it earlier and planned to do it without the kids. I'm going to trim the jib-sheet very flat and start luffing. You all right?'

She wasn't all right, she was scared, for she had been reading up sailing, and she knew that when it was not easy to sail safely, you luffed. Also, it was windier out here, there were quite big waves. However, she forced herself to call back, 'Aye, sir.'

He appreciated it. He reassured her, 'You'll be all right, A.B.'

They skimmed successfully past the headland, sometime within inches of the cliff, then the small cove was opening up, and David was pushing into it, which was quite a job, for the small half moon had more rocks to it than sand.

First thing he secured the boat very carefully. Then he came back and lifted her up and carried her through the creamy water to the beach.

Although they had not been out long she felt sea-heavy, and when he let her go she stumbled, and he came quickly back.

He held her to steady her, and she was suddenly sharply aware of his hard tough man strength, she could smell the male scent of him beneath the wet cotton of his shirt. She could feel the wet cotton against her own soaked blouse.

Then she was feeling hard salted lips on hers.

Knowing ... but not doing anything about it ... her own instinctive response.

CHAPTER NINE

Two days later they were back at Universe. On the evening of the curtailed sail, rain had started. All at once the bright skies had held a mild grievance in the form of a small grey cloud but one that had grown bigger even as you watched it.

'It's a warning,' Mr. Jones of the store had said when Catty had called in for provisions. She had collected them single-handed, David Jasper had sat stonily behind the wheel waiting for her.

It had only been an hour after they had put into the little cove, but now they withdrew angrily from each other.

Looking back, Catty shivered at that moment on the beach when finally she had stepped away from David's hard strong arms. Still dazed, she had looked wonderingly at him, wondering how it all had happened, for he had challenged and disliked and regretted her right from the first. She had disliked him, so how . . .

Her wonder must have reached him, for he had looked directly at her, and, suddenly embarrassed, not wanting him to think that she had taken the moment seriously, not when it could mean nothing to him, not after the attitude he always had adopted, she had stammered, 'There must be something about the sea. First Bevan, now—'

She had been going to say 'Now you', but she had been stopped by the quick anger in his eyes. Never had she seen such cold dislike.

'Collecting hearts like seashells. Is that what you mean, Sister Quentin?'

'I didn't mean that,' she had called back, 'but it will do.'

'Not for me. I don't get taken up and then discarded.'

'I thread my shells on a string,' she dared, so furious with him she could have stepped forward and hit him. She had been offering him a way out, an assurance of non-involvement – after all, he must have been as embarrassed as she had been, but he was flinging back the offer. She knew he could not possibly have been serious over that instinctive embrace, so, if her excuse of the sea was not accepted, he must mean it had been only an amusement, a diversion. She felt her cheeks burn.

She had turned to walk back down the beach, but he had crossed over and whirled her round to him.

'First Bevan,' he had demanded. 'What does that mean?'

'What does it sound like?'

'Answer me, damn you!'

'Why should I? On your own words you're only a member of and not the Board. Anyway, this is a private matter. Universe doesn't come into it.'

'Answer me, Catriona. What did you mean by "first Bevan"?'

'He proposed to me,' she said coolly. 'Now can I walk home?'

'What did you say to him?'

'Will you please let me go?'

'What did you say?'

'Doctor Jasper, take your hand off my shoulder!'

'If I do I'll shake the breath out of you until you answer, you damn girl!'

'I said no,' she said with a casualness she did not feel. 'The same as I would say to you if you asked.'

'Because there's nothing left for you to give? Because it was all used up? Non-involvement, that was what you always wanted, wasn't it?'

'Oh, you fool,' she had called, 'can't you see that that was what I was just offering you?'

'You flatter yourself,' he had said hatefully. He had made sure the boat held to the beach, then returned to her side. As they had climbed over the bordering rocks to the long beach, he had lent no helping hand. Exhausted from the few unnerving moments in the boat, after what had happened when they had scraped in, she had tripped and stumbled on her own behind him.

They had spoken little after that. To her inquiry about the boat, he had said he would see to it later. To his inquiry as to whether she needed groceries tonight she had said yes, but she could attend to that herself.

'I'll pick up the car and drive you there.'

'No need.'

'I will, though. It's going to rain. In fact it's going to deluge.' He had looked estimatingly at the sky.

'One cloud,' she had demeaned.

But Mr. Jones had said the same as David Jasper, and by the time they had returned to Blue Peter the grey warning had come true, and the entire sky was a menacing black mass. Looking back at the sea, Catty had seen that there was a deepening rush in the water now, that the waves, in spite of the protective reef, had angry crests. Presently it had started to rain.

And such rain! It had cut down in javelin-like drops, it had hit out at them as they had run from the car into the house.

At once Catty had counted the children. All present. She had set about tea, but heavily, almost as if she was still sea-heavy as she had been when she had stepped from the boat.

Everything went wrong. The toast burned. The eggs and milk ... scrambled eggs again by popular vote ... curdled. Mr. Jones's apricot jam, also by popular vote, turned out to be melon, which nobody liked. The rain leaked inside in quite a few places, and when Catty put out saucers to catch it, it made a dismal plop. David Jasper made no attempt to help out, he took a book and went to his room.

Catty got out Ludo and Snakes and Ladders, but everyone preferred to argue. There is nothing, she knew, as disenchanted as a seaside cottage in the rain. The girls were disenchanted.

The final straw was Ann Mary's shrill: 'Sister Pussycat, why don't you be like other ladies and go to work instead of always playing with us?'

It should have been funny, but Catty could not smile.

It rained all that night. She had to bring the beds in from the verandahs and put the children on the floor. The next day there were so many pools of water you did not know where the sea began.

It pelted every minute of that day, the sort of rain even oilskins can't deal with, and the girls only had plastic coats.

She kept them in, and it was sheer torment. The rain never stopped its cannonade, you had to shout to be heard. Why, thought Catty, don't I go to work like other ladies like Ann Mary said? I must be quite mad.

The rain shrieked all that next night, but in the morning the cannonade was not so pronounced. But it had a more set-in quality, and when David Jasper concurred with Mr. Jones that it was going to keep on, Catty agreed that they pack up and go. The children were not reluctant, they had gone through the indoor games that Catty had brought over a hundred times, and though Doctor David had remarked over breakfast that the paper reported state-wide rain, at least at Universe they had the library, the recreation room, their own private pursuits to follow.

David looked up the trains and connecting bus, then invited Catty without any show of enthusiasm to travel with him in the car.

'I'd better superintend the girls.'

'Why don't you say you'd sooner superintend the girls?'

'I would sooner superintend the girls,' she complied.

But she selected several of them, the ones likely to wander off, or linger behind, to travel with him, and with her lightened load of the more amenable ones caught the railway bus at the store in pelting rain and arrived at the station still in a downpour. It rained to Sydney, then it rained to Emu Heights. From beginning to end it was a dismal journey.

The Universe bus was there to meet them, and Ben said gravely that the riverlanders beneath the heights were becoming concerned.

'We're not very happy ourselves, Sister, although we're high, we're still in an indentation.'

'Yes,' said Catty, 'a kind of saucer. But' . . . looking out of the window . . . 'it does appear to be getting brighter, Ben.'

'It's the build-up,' gloomed the driver. 'The creeks were well fed with that freak snow and didn't need this extra.'

Coming into Universe was like coming home. Visibly, spirits soared, and Catty decided she would not go to work like other ladies after all but keep on stopping here to play with little girls. Now she found she could smile over that. The children, back in familiar surroundings, were sweet. Ann Mary, who had worried her with her over-possessiveness, had switched comfortably to Gwendolen. Gwendolen was most unmistakably becoming a different girl . . . *and Adrienne was going home.*

Catty had never felt more pleased. She had sensed the deep resentment Adrienne had felt when the desperate father, left when his wife had deserted him to cope alone, had kept his sons but boarded his daughter. He had done it for her good, but how could you tell a child that?

Now Adrienne was joining the family once more, because a good housekeeper had been found, a kindly-natured person who had asked for the return of the daughter of the house so as to make a happy unit again. The only thing that Catty dreaded were those empty looks on her children's faces as one of them . . . *but not them* . . . went a happy way. She planned a party when they came back to Sky House after farewelling Adrienne.

They all waved Adrienne down the drive, Belinda, who had featured in the worm episode, who featured in every episode with every girl because Belinda was like that, racing after the car to shout fond ... and desperately jealous, Catty suspected ... goodbyes.

'Darlings,' Catty called, 'there's lemonade and cake!'

They returned silently beside her, accepting their fate as such children learn to. But once inside Sky House they shouted in delighted surprise. Catty had bought goodies, but she had not got as far as a large box of chocolates ... *and a record player!* Beside the player was a pile of records, from nursery rhymes to suit Ann Mary and her contemporaries to pops for the older girls. Beside it all stood David Jasper.

'You shouldn't,' said Catty, as excited and happy herself.

'Say "No" to everything now,' he commented drily, taking up a record to play it.

'Oh, don't let's argue,' she entreated. 'I'm far too pleased to argue.'

'Then don't let us argue,' he nodded. He smiled suddenly. He had a very dear smile.

'Poor Adrienne,' pitied Belinda, 'she's missed this.'

Catty tried to thank him later, but he brushed the thanks aside. 'Don't you think I see their faces, too?' he reproached. 'Then remember, Sister, I was an "unbelonging" as well.' He looked at her oddly a moment. 'We've never talked about that, have we? About our mutual beginnings?'

'It's a long way back,' she said. 'Besides, I had a happy ending.'

'*Did* you?' he asked keenly. 'Are you sure of that? Sometimes I think—'

'I did,' she said a little fiercely. She had had a wonderful girlhood with Mother and Roger, and she refused to let her longing now for Gaby and Georgie to creep in and mar the memory.

'Catriona,' he said quietly and unexpectedly, 'have you anything to tell me?'

'Tell you . . . oh, yes, thanks, a million thanks. We will all delight in the player. But I'm afraid you must have deprived yourself.'

'I didn't mean that. I meant' . . . a pause . . . 'to do with – children.'

'Children?' She stared bewildered at him. 'They're all children. But you mean Gwendolen, of course. Gwendolen is a different girl now.'

'I wasn't thinking of Gwendolen, but since you have brought Gwendolen up, the Graces have pulled strings and used influences, and she can go home.'

'No,' said Catty.

'No? But home is the right place.'

'Not just yet. Oh, I can't explain it, and I expect I have no right, but I want to talk to them first. I—'

'But the talking is always done with parents of children like Gwendolen by people qualified to talk. You are not.'

She was silent.

'You want to keep Gwendolen a little longer, don't you?'

'Yes. You see, Ann Mary—'

'It's not Ann Mary.' He shook his head. 'Deep down in you, you want to keep her longer – to punish them.'

'No . . . I mean . . . of course not . . . well – well, I suppose so. They may have been all you told me, being the gifted pair they are they may have had demands made on them, but—'

'But the understanding of a child is a bigger demand, Sister Quentin.' He quoted what she once had said.

'I think so.' She did not look at him.

'Do you know what? I think so, too.' She had not expected that, and she turned in surprise, and once more he was smiling . . . and he had a dear smile.

'But,' he said, 'keep your sticky little fingers out of what doesn't concern you, Sister Quentin. *I* will have that talk.'

'Professionally or old boys together? Also, it does concern me.'

'You have no right to be answered, but I'll answer you. It will be professionally as well as students, not boys, Sister Quentin, together. I happen to have a psychology degree as well as a medical.'

'No wonder the bush can't hope to keep you,' she tossed angrily, angry at the quick change of him, one minute agreeing with her, the next laying down a law.

'Did you want to?' he asked. He put it so mildly, so inconsequentially, that she didn't consider it needed an answer, and yet, as he still waited, she felt a pulse starting to beat in her temple, and she hoped he did not notice. Do I want him here? – Yes, I do. *I do.*

He was waiting no longer. 'So please leave this to me,' he said.

'Yes, sir.' – Was he noticing that pulse?

'Sister Quentin, are you all right?'

'Yes, sir.'

'No need to be impertinent.'

'I thought I was being polite, sir.'

'You're a wretch of a girl.'

'Yes, sir.'

He looked as though he was going to step forward, he even made a spontaneous move, then he said, 'Well, if you've no other answer—'

'Than yes, sir?'

'Than what I asked you and you promptly interpreted as dealing with Gwendolen.'

'I don't understand you, sir.'

'If you say that once more I'll—'

'I won't, Doctor Jasper. I really did think you referred to Gwendolen. I'll keep my sticky fingers out of your business, but can I at least pass the time of day with the Graces when they visit on Saturday? After all, I am house-mother.'

'You're Sister Pussycat, but you have the claws of a tiger. Now I'm going to read Chapter Fifteen in spite of the record player, I have to know the end of Fourteen myself, so you can fulfil your rendezvous with Bruce.'

'I met him once,' she said wearily. 'Will I call the young female busybodies with their insatiable personal curiosity and their cool controlled calculating minds?'

With that sudden change he could adopt he grinned at her. 'Remember what I say, don't you?'

'I don't, I mean—'

'You do. It's word for word. Our first meeting. Chapter and verse.' He looked deeply at her. 'Catriona ... Catriona, I still feel there's something you might want to tell me ... ask me ...'

'I want to tell you I'm taking the usual walk I take when you read to the girls. I want to ask if it's all right.'

'It's all right, and I hope you fall over the cliff!' he snapped.

'I'll see what I can do,' she promised, and went out into the late spring night.

The Graces arrived on visiting day in their own car. They had left their other children at home to make room for Gwendolen and her bags.

Catty was not present when David Jasper delivered his little speech, so she could not judge whether it had been old students together style or strictly a psychological discourse. But whatever it was, it was successful, for the Graces agreed to go back without their daughter, and since the idea of her being 'placed' in Universe, even though it was a better step than where she was before, must have grieved them, Catty considered that David must have said some telling things.

Gretel Grace admitted this later to Catty over a private cup of tea in Sky House, the girls ... and Gwendolen ... were attending the visitors at their tea in Horizon Hall, so Gretel and Catty could talk without fear of being overheard.

It was a little face-losing to Catty to find that Gretel

was really sweet. Her keen clever face with the bright alert eyes was the face of a mother as well as a scholar, and just now a saddened mother.

'I've never understood Gwendolen, not like the others. Oh, don't think I've been unkind, I believe if anything Hugo and I have indulged her, but there must have been something she saw in us, a little unconscious impatience, perhaps, because her intelligence—'

'Ran in different channels,' broke in Catty. She related in detail the intuition and imagination that must have prompted Gwendolen to divert and amuse a child instead of prevailing upon her so that a frightening situation had ended instead on a happy note. 'On a very happy note,' related Catty. She told Gretel about Ann Mary's adoration. 'To see Gwendolen's pleasure is very satisfying,' she smiled.

'Gwendolen has the second brother and her sister younger than her, but there has never been that older sister feeling with them. I always thought it was because—'

'Because they knew the answers quicker than Gwendolen,' said Catty.

'Well – they *are* very bright.'

'In certain things. Has it ever occurred to you that Gwendolen is bright in things that they are not, things for instance that take time to complete, to round and mould and perfect. Your other children, I believe, have mercury brains ... they grasp quickly and accurately. But Gwendolen feels words and colours and shape, she has dreams, and perhaps words and colours and shapes and dreams don't change a nation, but—'

'You shame me – my own daughter a poet?'

'It could be an artist, it could be a dozen things, but because it's not facts, mathematical facts, scientific facts, you—'

'I've been an intolerant parent. Oh, I haven't shown it, but she's sensed it, sensed her exclusion, then in desperation she has tried to break through, to make us aware of her, by doing what she did.'

'She won't again,' said Catty. 'Up here she feels important. The girls were all impressed by the incident I told you, and Ann Mary—'

'Yes,' said Gretel thoughtfully, 'Ann Mary—'

The Graces departed with the other visitors, and Catty, watching Gwendolen closely, saw a relaxation in the girl that had not been there when she first had come to Universe.

'I can go home whenever I like,' she told Catty, 'and I will, only not just yet. You see, Ann Mary – well, Ann Mary—'

Ann Mary. Catty did not know about Ann Mary's mother because there was nothing on the notes that Mr. Chester had supplied about the mother, but she did know, and she had met, her grandmother. 'She has the same face as you.'

Perhaps Gwendolen with her finer senses sensed that Ann Mary was going to need her, because that night when David Jasper came across to Sky House he had the reason why Ann Mary's grandmother had not been among the day's visitors. Ann Mary's grandmother had died.

'Oh . . .' said Catty, feeling she did not know how to handle this. She was thinking of those breathless sobs. 'Has she *anyone*?'

'All we know is that her mother brought Ann Mary home to her grandmother, then left.'

'Then she is unbelonging?'

'Well – she is now.'

'What do you mean?' Catty looked at him inquiringly.

'I don't know yet. But we won't fret the child by telling her, not for a while. For one thing I'm going to be far too busy to rush up to Universe to sedate an emotional upset. Perhaps you don't know it, but the flats are expecting floods.'

'Floods? But it's stopped raining . . . well, heavy rain,

anyway.'

'For another thing,' he said, 'I wouldn't be surprised if—' He did not finish, though, he returned instead to the expected floods.

'There's been a minor fall every day for weeks, there's been no absolute let-up, no time for absorption or drying out. The creeks swollen from the freak snow have been building up, and they've rushed down to overflow the river weir. That weir was never built for anything like it's getting now.'

'Have there been floods before?'

'Only river spillovers that the farmers have actually gained from, for the spillovers leave precious topsoil silt, and are manageable, anyway. But never a weir overflow, and a possible weir collapse, as is threatening now.'

'What will happen?'

'Parts of the flats will be isolated. We can tell which parts, and already the authorities are shifting out the families who will go. But of course a lot won't go, and can you blame them? It's their home, and until the overflow actually laps at the door . . .' He sighed. 'It will be a heli-copter job then.'

'Will down there be cut off from Universe?' She really meant 'Will *you*?' but she carefully did not say it.

'Completely. At the foot of Universe hill there's a kind of indentation, or selection of low terrain, almost a hollow or sunken portion, before the slopes and river flats set in, and that indentation will prevent any road com-munication between here and the plain. Incidentally, this plateau might catch a bit of flood, too, as it's also set rather saucer-wise, but still, being high, it must naturally have a run-off, so you needn't worry so long as you don't get in the way of any angry runnel or swollen creek.'

'I won't,' she said. She asked if she could do any-thing.

'Just hope you don't have an emergency, that's all, but if you do, keep a cool head.'

'I would, anyway, but I really meant could I do anything for you?'

'For me?' He stood looking down at her so long that at last she stammered, 'I meant, of course, for the threatened flats. Can I help you in the trouble you anticipate?'

'No,' he said . . . and still looked at her.

Before he left he took her across to the hospital and went through the medicines with her. Everything seemed to be on hand, from simple medicants to the modern antibiotics. But no anaesthetic. Who would need an anaesthetic?

The next day school was closed. The surrounding creeks were rising so quickly it was feared the little building could be isolated and the children marooned in the space of a few learning hours.

Catty took the news thankfully, for though the track down to Emu Heights from the Camp was a high dry one, she knew the ways of the young, the heady delight of launching bark boats, throwing in twigs and leaves, then following the stream to see where the boats had sailed. Safe in Sky House, she had no fears for them, even if she did miss out on her precious nine-to-four respite from shrill little voices and endless demands.

She insisted that they formed a class and did their schooling as usual, and for a while the novelty of lessons at home kept them absorbed. It also discovered a perfect teacher-to-be in Dorothea, previously rather a scatter-brained girl, who took over the superintending as though she had a teacher's diploma. It was strange, Catty mused, how a child's talent can hide under a bushel and then suddenly arise and you see clearly what the child can, and should, be. Dorothea had never shown any inclination to lead, not educationally, but in front of the improvised class she fell naturally into the role of schoolroom supervisor. No one thought to question her right of quietening them, telling them when they could put their books down, take them up again. A teacher in

Dorothea. An artist or an author or something delicate and dedicated in Gwendolen. A nurse in Anne.

A nurse in Anne. How valuable Catty was to find that gift within the next twenty-four hours.

She took the children out for a quick breath of fresh air in the late afternoon; there was only a Scotch mist of rain, so their plastic coats could cope.

There was nothing spectacular to look at, just the usual wet weather puddles. Even from the look-out, as they called the highest point of Universe, there wasn't anything to see. The river below was a bright yellow, but it did not appear particularly menacing. They went across for tea, then back to Sky House, then had an hour of records as there would be no chapter tonight on Bettina, then went to bed.

Catty did not know how long she had slept when the insistent tap on the door woke her up. It was Anne, and Catty's first thought was that the girl was ill. But she was dressed, fully dressed. She also had on her little cap.

'What is it, Anne?'

'Mr. Williams came across, there's an emergency come in, Sister Pussycat. We have to go over to the hospital ... I mean you have to ...' Anne looked anxiously at Catty.

'We have to,' Catty said, 'but, darling, how do you know so quickly – was I sleeping heavily and Tony ... Mr. Williams couldn't wake me up?'

'No, I got up before he knocked. I had a feeling, Sister, a nursing-sort of feeling – oh, I can't tell you, but I had to get up.'

Catty said nothing; she could find no words. When she did find them, finding her clothes and scrambling into them hurriedly, she asked, 'Did Tony say what it was.'

Anne answered calmly: 'A baby.'

'A – a what?'

'It's a Mrs. Brennan from the river bend up at Felix Park.'

'But she can't come here!'

'She can't go anywhere else. She was evacuated, but she came back, and when her husband went to take her in again, he couldn't get through. The only place he could get her was here. If the baby waits till the morning, Doctor David can come in by air, but the helicopter couldn't land tonight. Are you ready, Sister Pussycat?'

Ready! Catty had never felt less ready in her life. She had had no obstetric training, indeed, all her training had been in children's wards, on children's complaints.

'It's a first baby,' Anne said as she led the way.

'Then it will take a while.' Thank heaven, thought Catty, for that; in the morning they could summon David and—

'It's already been a while,' Anne said.

'How – how do you know all this? Oh, from Mrs. Chester.' Dear Mrs. Chester. Mrs. Chester, who had had a family. With Mrs. Chester beside her—

'But the Chesters aren't here,' said Anne. 'Didn't you know? They went down for supplies late yesterday afternoon, and now, because all the creeks have risen, they can't get back.'

'Then – then who is there?'

'You will be, Sister, and if I can help—'

'Oh, darling, I do appreciate you, but this is a baby, not – not barley broth. I mean, Anne, we all had that talk that day, but there's much more to it than that, than what I told you, and Anne, you're too young.'

'I'm not, Sister Pussycat. Oh, I know I am really, but I'm not inside. I know a lot, and if you'll just tell me more, then tell me what to do—'

'I hope neither of us have to do.' They had reached the sick bay, and Catty, followed by Anne, stepped inside.

The young husband was talking with Tony, and as they entered he came apologetically across.

'This is an imposition, I know it, but it's Janet's first, and I guess she wanted to remain with me to the last moment – I mean it's naughty of her, but you do see—'

'Yes,' Catty assured him, 'I see, but—' She stopped herself at that; no use to have a husband on her hands as well as his wife.

She went into the little ward.

Janet was sitting on the bed and looking supremely unperturbed. If you knew how I was shaking, thought Catty, you wouldn't be calm like that. She took a deep breath to steady herself, then asked Janet questions.

Yes, she had had pains. She recounted them, and their number and length did not cheer Catty.

Had Doctor set a date? Last week, smiled Janet. She did not help by confiding that she had not kept to Doctor's diet so would probably have a large child.

'Which is suitable for a farmer,' she tossed with a laugh.

Catty did not laugh.

She asked Janet about natural birth. No, she hadn't trained for it, actually, Sister, she hadn't had time, a mixed farm wife had all her hours occupied. – Like mine are going to be now, Catty knew.

She took Janet's temperature, checked her pulse, said she could talk to her husband for a while, then she went outside with Ann. Tony had gone back to his house and she did not blame him, but she did envy him ... quite fiercely.

'Anne,' she said, 'I want you to listen.'

'Yes, Sister Pussycat.'

'This is what's going to happen. I don't want you to be startled.'

'I won't, Sister.'

She explained everything, and as she did a calmness seemed to take over. It was because, she thought, this is not a fifteen-year-old I'm talking to, it's a fine, serene, matured, dependable woman.

'There's no anaesthetic, Anne, should we need it, so the important thing is to have the mother relax.'

'Relax,' nodded Anne.

Catty got up and went back to the ward. She told Anne to help Janet out of her clothes.

She set Jim making coffee, then when they had all had a cup she talked with Janet again, timed her, and knew most certainly that this baby would not wait for a helicopter in the morning.

'I think,' said Janet a little tightly, 'it could be soon.'

Catty nodded for Anne to slip behind Janet and take her wrists, then she went out and asked Jim to go across to Tony. She made up some sort of message, anything to get him away, for there wasn't anything to give Janet, and if the baby was big . . .

When she came back, Anne was saying, 'Big breaths. Look, I'll breathe with you. That's the girl!'

Janet gave a shudder and said, 'I could do with a whiff right now.'

'What for?' said Anne. 'When it's here?'

'Here?'

'Just one minute . . . one minute more . . . one minute . . . Sister Pussycat, Sister, it *is*!'

And it was. Before she could do the necessary things, *Anne* was doing them, Anne rising fifteen, Anne who would leave here next month and go into a factory, or keep house for her mother, or— Anne was busy on the umbilical cord Catty had told her about, she was inclining the tiny one back to help him cry, she was reaching for a soft clean towel, covering him again in a warm rug. She was saying to the astonished mother: 'You have a farmer.'

'Is he?' asked Janet dazedly. 'Then he's Giles. Farmer Giles. – Oh, where's Jim?'

The baby was sleeping. The mother was sleeping. Jim was drinking a celebration coffee with Catty. Anne, who had said to Catty as they had cleared up: 'It's funny, Sister Pussycat, but I don't seem worried any more, I don't think I ever will be again, it was wonderful, *I* feel wonderful,' had gone to the door to look out into the night, then, as more light had crept into the sky . . . had all those hours gone since Anne had wakened her up,

Catty wondered? . . . had stepped outside.

Inside, the mother and baby still slept, Catty and Jim still talked softly together . . . and then the wall of water struck.

Fortunately it missed the hospital, missed all the Universe buildings, the swollen remnant of water that had escaped its creek's banks and come swirling instead across the Camp to lose itself again down the valley missed the gardens, the grove, the children's playground and the new cricket pitch that Tony had laid down.

But it caught Anne. It took Anne. By the time that Jim and Catty ran out, Anne was beyond their reach. If Anne had stepped out one minute before, one minute after, to look up into the first light and smile . . . for Catty knew she would be smiling . . . at all that had happened, at the lovely miracle of it, at her particular miracle, she would have been here. One minute before, one minute after. Catty knew she would remember that all her life.

At eight o'clock Tony came in at last to tell Catty that they had found Anne. No, he said gently to her mute question, no, Sister. He said that it had been so quick, so sudden, she would never have known.

He said that there was no danger of any more creek diversions. He said that the position on the riverlands had eased. He told her that the phone was functioning again.

It was David Jasper who spoke when Catty picked up the receiver in answer to its ring.

'Yes,' she said dully in reply to his inquiry if she was all right.'

'I've been worried,' he said almost roughly. 'I haven't stopped all night, emergencies everywhere, but every minute of the time—'

'We had a baby.' Still dully. 'Mrs. Brennan of Felix Park. A boy.'

'All well?'

'Yes.'

'That's great.'

As if a long way off, much further than down the valley, Catty heard him praising her. Praising *her*? It should be Anne.

'David—' she broke in. Something in her voice must have reached him. There was a pause.

'Yes, Sister Pussycat?' he asked.

'Anne,' she whispered.

'Yes?'

'We've – lost her.'

Another pause from David. Then: 'Ann Mary? Anne with an E?'

'Anne,' she said, and then the tears that had not come before were racking her, and David Jasper was saying quietly yet strongly, his voice reaching across the wire and holding her: 'I'll come at once.'

In five minutes the surplus water had escaped from Universe plateau down to the valley, and in five days the inundated riverlands had drained away. The only evidence of what had happened were piles of debris caught against the flood levels, wrecked gardens, uprooted trees . . . and an ache in the heart for Anne. She had been the only loss. Ironic, knew Catty, that on the plateau, the safe high place, a girl had drowned.

Anne's mother had arrived, decked out in expensive black. She had cried expansively, wondered how she could meet expenses, she wanted everything nice for Anne, and when David Jasper said quietly that there would be no expenses for her to meet, the crying had stopped as something else was wondered by Anne's mother. 'She was to support me,' she said. 'I'm not getting younger, and she was ready for work.'

But not for nursing, sorrowed Catty's heart, you deprived her of that. She remembered Anne those last few minutes saying: 'It's funny, Sister, but I don't seem worried any more, I don't think I ever will be again, it was wonderful, I feel wonderful!' Oh, Anne, Nurse Anne.

'Everything will be gone into,' David assured the mother.

The next evening he came across for Chapter Seventeen. 'No,' he told Catty, 'it never ends, it's a spaceship Peyton Place. Also, this is only the first book of a series.'

'All with Bettina?'

'If it helps I'll alter the name.'

'It doesn't matter.' She laughed, and knew it was the first time for days. She must try to laugh. With children there had to be smiles.

'Only,' she continued, 'it would be awkward if we got a Bettina – not awkward, really, but contentious, there wouldn't be a girl who didn't envy her the name. And we'll be having a new girl.' She stopped abruptly, thinking again of Anne.

'We'll be having three,' David said.

'Three?'

'One replacing Anne,' he said firmly. 'One replacing Gwendolen, one for Ann Mary.'

'Ann Mary? I knew Gwendolen would be going, but Ann Mary – Where?'

'With Gwendolen,' he said. As she stood incredulous, he explained, 'I rather thought it might happen after our talk with the Graces. They're intelligent people and they could see that to part this rather odd couple now—'

'But do they *want* her?'

'As much as they want Gwendolen, and I can tell you that that wanting could fill the world. So' . . . he looked consideringly at Catty, almost as though he was thinking out something, a right moment, a right approach . . . 'we have one space to fill.'

'Three spaces.'

'One. – The others have been settled.' He was still looking consideringly at her.

'What are their ages?' she asked automatically.

'Seven and five.'

Seven and five . . . Gaby's and Georgie's ages.

'Orphans?'

'Father dead.'

'Mother?'

"Doesn't want them any more.'

She nodded sadly. 'It'll be difficult, the unwanted ones are always the hardest.'

'Not in this case. They want to come.'

'Have they heard of Universe?'

'No . . . but they've heard of you.'

'Of me?' She looked at him in confusion. 'Who has heard of me?' she asked.

'Gabrielle Forbes, Georgina Forbes. If you want a description I'll give it to you. Look, I'll even show you their photos.' He handed across Catty's lost leather wallet.

'Where – where did you get this?'

'I rescued it just before a small girl threw it across the cliff.'

'Ann Mary?'

'Yes.'

'She was jealous,' said Catty.

'Not half as jealous as I was.'

As she stared at him, he said, 'Oh, not of the kids, they'd always been mine as well.' – *His* as well? – 'But of the father of them, the dead father. I was ready to fight a living memory, Catriona, but how could I fight one that was gone?'

'Roger was my brother, my darling brother . . . oh, I know he wasn't really, but he was *actually* to me. I adored Gaby and Georgie. When Lilla took them away . . .' She stopped, puzzled. 'You just said you weren't jealous of the children, they had always been yours as well.'

'That's true. Lilla was my foster-sister, her family adopted me. I thought she was the sun, moon and stars. When she went to England and married there, it was a wrench, and I used to live for word of her. When she sent me photos of the girls . . . these girls . . . they were mine, just as you believed they were yours.'

'But you hate all females.'

'For a while I did. I worshipped Lilla, you see, and she

184

let me down.'

'You loved her? You didn't want her to marry?'

'No, nothing like that. It was her slip from the pedestal on which I had put her. For a long time when her letters came, her uncaring, cruel letters, I blamed her husband. I told myself that he had made her like that. But somewhere deep down in me I knew that Lilla had always been like that, only I would never recognize it, that it was not this man. Then he died, and she remarried at once. She wrote saying that the kids would be off her hands at last. I think that did it. I hated all women, little women, big women, young and old . . . except my two.'

'*My* two,' Catty corrected.

'Ours.'

There was a pause.

'I lost track of Lilla . . . I didn't want to remember her . . . then one day I had a quick glimpse of your photos as you shut them up. I wasn't sure, but I know a finger touched my heart. Since then I've been tracking Lilla, and it's only been recently that we've been in touch.'

'And what about the girls?' she asked.

'In a school, from the sound of it *not* so good.' His lip curled. 'The second marriage had failed. Lilla was on the move again. She rushed my offer to have them out here.'

'She wouldn't have had she known I was here as well.'

'I told her. I told her the children would not be mine, but ours.'

'Lilla accepted that?'

There was a silence, and in the silence Catty could see the man fighting a contempt that was stifling him. Then he said: 'She would do anything for money.'

'You – you bought them?'

'You could say that,' he nodded, 'you could say I bought Gaby and Georgie.'

'But – but I have no money to buy my share of them.' She looked at him pitifully.

There was another silence, the longest of all, and then David said: 'Perhaps I could buy you.'

'Do – do you want to?'

'Not particularly. I would prefer exchange.'

'Exchange?'

'Of love.'

'Love?' she said softly.

'Love. Ever heard of it? Apart from children ... apart from meetings under orange trees ... apart from – Catriona, apart from these, have you heard of love?'

'Yes.'

'But do you have love? *That* love?'

'Yes.'

'In spite of my gibes against Bevan, have you love for him?'

'No.'

'For anyone else? Tony? One of the riverland men?'

'No.'

'For anyone at all?'

'Yes.'

'Who?'

'You,' she said.

He did not come across to her at once, first he said cautiously: 'You're saying that to get the children. You needn't, you know, I'll play fair.'

'How generous! Wouldn't it have been better to have said that in the beginning than to have embarrassed me into saying what I did?'

'Did it embarrass you?'

'Yes ... no. I mean—'

'What do you mean?'

'I mean that you must be pleased now that you've humbled me, now that you've—' But she said no more, she was in his arms.

'I love you, you bumbled woman, I love you to the ends of the earth. I loved you the first moment I saw you. I hated you, too ... yes, I admit that ... because for the first time I knew I was wrong in what I had become

186

through Lilla. I can love you *with* our children or *without* our children, but it had better be with, Catriona, because they're expected at any minute. In fact if you look through the door . . .'

It was true. *It was true.* The bus was panting up the drive. Two little figures were getting out, and she was running to them.

'Darlings, darlings!'

'Aunty Catty!'

'Here they say Sister Pussycat,' said David by Catty's side, 'you'll soon learn. You don't know me. I'm David.'

'Uncle David,' said Catty.

They were crossing to Sky House, the four of them, and the other children were standing at the door, sizing them up.

Then Teacher Dorothea was taking over. She was saying, 'Doctor David, if you and Sister Pussycat want to settle in the new ones, I'll read Chapter Seventeen.'

'No,' refused David, 'I wouldn't miss it for the world.'

But as he took out the book he gave Catty a look that said that chapters finish, that children are bedded, that the night goes on after lights go out.

Catty went into the garden . . . Gaby and Georgie already in the spaceship with Bettina and the others . . . and waited deliriously.

As David shut the book and called, 'Go before you get into bed, and that means you two as well, Gaby and George,' she heard Ann Mary . . . it was always Ann Mary . . . asking: 'Why is a girl George?'

have you heard about Harlequin's great new series?

Harlequin Presents

*ANNE HAMPSON
*ANNE MATHER
*VIOLET WINSPEAR

These three very popular Harlequin authors have written many outstanding romances which we have not been able to include in the regular Harlequin Series.

Now we have made special arrangements to publish many of these delightful never — before — available stories in a new author series, called "Harlequin Presents".

See following page for complete listing of titles available.

Have You Missed Any of These
Harlequin Romances?

All books are 60c. Please use the handy order coupon.

NN